"*I am Leonard* is several of my favorite dystopian nightmares rolled into one, narrated by the heroic love child of Scrooge and the Grinch."

- LEOD FITZ, AUTHOR OF *THE CORPSE-EATER SAGA*

"Sorry, Will Smith. Richter penned the perfect homage to Matheson's *I am Legend*."

- BRIAN KAUFMAN, AUTHOR OF *DEAD BEYOND THE FENCE*

Praise for *L.I.F.E. in the 23rd Century_*

'Satire is a dying art in the USA, so consider this novel an endangered species. If Monty Python adopted a chimp and read it 1984 as a bedtime story, this is what it would dream.'

- AARON SPRIGGS, AUTHOR OF *THE STRANGE AND SAVAGE LIFE OF A BRASSKEY JOURNALIST*

I AM LEONARD

I AM LEONARD

AND OTHER STORIES

JASON R. RICHTER

Dedicated to everyone that continues to support this type of behavior.
Specifically, Paul for the profanity and McKinney for the motivation.

CONTENTS

ALSO BY JASON R. RICHTER_

L.I.F.E. in the 23rd Century

PUBLISHING HISTORY_

"The White Elephant." First published in The Mountain
Scribes Anthology.
    2009

"Pictographology." First published in Crossed Genres, Issue
21, "Invasion."
    August, 2010

"The Fortress of Evil." First published in the *Probing Uranus*
anthology as "The Continuing Adventures of Agent Jonas
Maxwell, Intergalactic Space Agency: "The Fortress of Evil.""
    2010

I AM LEONARD

AND OTHER STORIES

I AM LEONARD

AND OTHER STORIES

JASON R. RICHTER

I am Leonard

The *Ishmael's* closest to my apartment now has a human barista sitting behind the counter. If this turns into an ongoing annoyance, I will take my business to the *Ishmael's* on the next block.

I didn't hear what the person at the front of the line said, but the barista leans into the microphone on the counter and repeats the order.

"Half-caff mocha," he said, his head bobbing to his affected cadence, "soy, whipped cream." He rises from his stool and shuffles in either a dance number or rhythmic seizure. "Half-caff-scoodle," he scatted, "mocha-broodle, soy-whip-froodle."

Third in line, I see the drink slide out of W.A.L.T., the coffee machine. "W.A.L.T. says your half-caff, soy, mocha with whip is ready. That's what W.A.L.T. says."

Yesterday, I walked up to the coffee machine and spoke

into the microphone myself. Today, the barista had a government grant to elevate everyone's experience.

He shuffled around a few more times, sat down, and handed the customer his drink. "Savor that, brother," said the barista. "Who else wants some?"

The next customer, a woman, mumbled her order to the barista.

"Coming right up, sister!" Into the microphone, he said, "Iced caramel macchiato, upside down with whipped cream." He went back into seizure mode when the machine had the order. "Caramel-froodle, macchi-scoodle, upside-doodle, whip-noodle."

The machine said, "W.A.L.T. says your iced caramel macchiato, upside down with whipped cream is ready. That's what W.A.L.T. says."

The drink slid out, but the barista repeated his jazz-scat, not once, but twice, before he handed the woman her drink. "Relish that, sweetheart," he said. She giggled, as she walked away.

"What do you desire, my friend?" he asked me.

Typically, I spend a half-hour in the coffee shop catching up on the news, before I leave for work. This idiot, with his scat and shuffle routine, had destroyed most of that time.

"Drip," I said.

"Excuse me?" he said.

"Say the word 'drip' into the microphone, so I can get my coffee and go."

He leaned forward. "Drip," he said into the microphone. He stood up to start dancing, but I raised my hand.

"Let me do it for you," I said. "Drip-doodle." I did a jumping jack.

"W.A.L.T. says your drip coffee is ready. That's what W.A.L.T. says."

"Can I have my coffee?" I asked.

He snorted and slid my cup across the counter. "What are you supposed to be, bro?"

"What do you mean?"

"What's the costume for, my dude?"

I looked down at my clothes, then around the room at everyone else. Sure, I was the only person wearing a tie and slacks. The only person who owned a shirt with sleeves, comb, and mirror. The only person who didn't look like a refugee from a post-apocalyptic action movie. But that was no reason to call my clothes a "costume."

"I'm on my way to work," I said.

He laughed. "No really, what's with the costume, homey?"

"I have an office job, and that's where I'm heading, after I finish my coffee."

"Whatever," he said. "If you aren't going to tell me, step aside for the next customer."

As I walked away, the Slam-Go app popped up on my phone –commanding me–to rate the interaction.

I chose Slam.

"The barista tried to be avant-garde but succeeded at being annoying. The jazz-scat he performed, as he served my coffee, was off-key, unnecessary, and stale."

That's what showed up on my screen, anyway. With the Sub-Vocalizer app activated, it sounded like I was trying to improve my gorilla impression, as I balanced my cup on my walk to a table. The Slam went directly to the barista's personal SpaceBook, the Jazz-Scat Barista Guild page, and Yarp! page for the café. His universal rating dutifully decreased.

Two other things happened when I sent the Slam.

1. Immediate attrition of the line in the coffee shop. People are willing to wait for a mediocre cup of corporate coffee, but not if the barista's jazz-scat is anything other than on-point.

2. The troll army in the ether began lambasting me for being judgmental, cold-hearted, and uninformed. You know, the usual troupe of bomb hurlers hiding safely behind their screen. There were only two noteworthy posts. One commented on the diminutive nature of my *"gennytallya,"* and the second assumed I was an ass-faced Red Sox fan—not that anyone had mentioned baseball—and hoped I would be *"mudred violetly."* As compared to chartreuse or yellowy, I suppose.

Ah, trolls. If you knew how to spell, your entertainment value would decrease exponentially.

Slam-Go was for "skin-to-skin" interactions only. Reviews couldn't be brigaded into submission. None of the anonymous horde could increase the barista's universal rating one dot unless they walked into the café and bought a cup of coffee from him. Most of them were cursing my name from a different continent. The flame war flickered out by the time I got my coffee from the counter to a table. It started and stopped in an instant, but not exactly instantly.

After a moment at the table, it sinks in that I should have ordered my coffee in a *Tug-O.* Just to my left, a poet waves his E-Quill, chanting the words, as he writes them in neon green in the air above his table. He is lean, in a twitchy sort of way. His hair is spiked into a matching neon green mohawk. He's wearing a tan shirt and black pants. The shirt's too tight, the pants too baggy. To my right, about five or six tables away is another air scribbler. He's shorter and more muscular than the other guy. He has the same clothing on, but in reverse—tan pants, black shirt. His hair is cut in two equal racing stripes, just above his ears. His hair and luminous squiggles from his E-Quill are hot, hot pink. Between the complimentary E-Quill colors, mirrored clothing, and one complete haircut between the two of them, it's surely a setup.

The crowd is enthralled. The poets' combined chanting builds like nuclear proliferation. Mohawk gets a little louder, then Racing Stripes gets a little louder than that. Then, Mohawk gets a little louder still. And on, and on.

And yawn.

And on, and on some more.

Mohawk shouts "Monkey goggles, pig knuckle," as he paints the words on the air in front of him.

Racing Stripes responds with, "Outcaster, hoodie whip," as he laces the air with letters. His strokes are huge.

A pause.

They stare each other down across the café. With a deep breath, they both shout, "Vagabond skeet farfle."

The crowd gasps. How could they both say the same random three words, everyone wondered?

Everyone, but me.

The poets charge at each other, stopping belly to belly, nose to nose. They shout gibberish into each other's faces, into each other's mouths. Right arms flail their words to the sky, from the top down. The older, higher words melt and dribble down onto the newer words. The men crouch down, as they write and scream, their noses always touching until they sit cross-legged, knee to knee, nose to nose.

And then, silence.

The piece of art rotates in a full circle for everyone to enjoy. It's a flaccid penis writ large complete with neon green pubes and sagging neon pink scrotum. The piece makes its single revolution, and the two men whisper, "Armistice."

Then, the drawing vanishes.

The coffee shop customers erupt in applause. Phones went into the air. The poets hold their own phones up, so they can catch the flung e-change from the adoring masses.

Their name is an animal, then a shape, I thought. Ever

since those idiots in *Antelope Disk* did a performance piece on Blu-Tube and won an Oscar, everyone has mimicked them.

Mohawk took a bow and said, "Thank you, so much."

With tears in his eyes, he thinks this is his one, big break. His elevation point.

Racing Stripes said, "We are *Cattle Sphere*."

I knew it.

Cheering increases as Slam-Go pops up on everybody's phones. I watch as the screen racks up emblazoned "Go" green lights, quintuple stars, and two thumbs way, way up.

And my one fist, Slam branded into the knuckles.

I take what's left of my coffee and make my way to the door. I'm about to take the last swallow when confetti cannons go off.

Someone actually brought confetti.

To a coffee shop.

That's brilliant.

I drop my cup of recycled, paper-flavored coffee into the bus tub.

I give humanity two thumbs way, way down.

CHAPTER TWO_

My footsteps echo through the empty lobby of the office building. Doors to the street swing closed, darkness envelopes me. I pause a beat to give the electric eye in the ceiling time to register my presence. Fluorescent bulbs buzz on to light the length of the corridor. Not that I need the light. Across the lobby to the stairway is a straight shot. Granted, it is a double football field length straight shot through an abandoned building. The main computer turning on the lights is more for my morale than for my navigation.

Each door I pass on the left and right is the same every morning. Office of Some-such, the County Clerk, Comptroller, City Manager. Every door has an electronic lock, its eye burned red in the half-light. When I first asked for my job, I read the legend on one of the locks.

Sealed by the Automation Act of 2115.

During my mandated breaks, I wander the halls, looking for a door with a green, instead of red eye. There aren't any. Six floors, 50 offices on each floor, nothing but red lights. Except mine.

When I reach the landing on the second floor, the voice

starts.

"You shouldn't be here," it whispers. "You should be with your own kind."

The voice is everywhere and nowhere, so faint that it could come from the end of the hallway or bottom of a trash can.

"Go from this place. The world is waiting for you." Etcetera. Etcetera.

Once on the sixth floor, I walk the length of the building again, back to the street side. Six flights of stairs vertically, four football fields horizontally.

Every morning.

Every lunch break.

Every night when I leave.

I can open a coconut with my thighs.

The voice persists as I make my way to my office, but I've heard the rote admonishments so many times that they blend with my footsteps.

"Leave while you still can," is always followed by, "Your life awaits you outside," and then, "Go, be free, and create beauty."

You get the idea.

The last door on the left is mine. I don't get a fancy, *Office of...* placard. Just plain, old *Data Services*.

Inside my office, a speaker on an articulated arm rests in front of the microphone for the building's paging system. "The destiny of mankind is art," comes from the speaker into the microphone.

"Morning, Walt," I said.

The arm moves, so the blue light in the speaker faces me. "Good morning, Jonas."

Walt is the main computer.

It's technically W.A.L.T.

World Automated = Leisure Time.

I work for the government entering applications for artistic grants. I am the government's only employee and the only worker in the world who doesn't have a job linked to my own artistic endeavors.

"Are you feeling well?" Walt asks.

"I'm fine, thanks for asking." I hang my jacket on the hook behind the office door.

"I only ask because it usually takes you less time to walk from the front door to the office." The speaker moves along a track in the ceiling, following me to my desk. "You are historically in the office well before I get to, 'The destiny of mankind is art.'"

My workstation's monitor winks on as I sit down, and the keyboard rises to rest under my fingers. Walt's "eye" is directly in front of me, awaiting a response.

"You could take the day off and paint a mural with butterflies," Walt suggests. "Didn't you once say that you like butterflies? Did you see what the President did over the weekend?"

The monitor changes from the data entry program to BluTube. A video showing the President giving a speech in the Rose Garden, his baggy coveralls riddled with paint splatters. The camera angle shifted to show the side of the White House, an abstract, neon mural covering the entire West Wing.

"Can I get to work, Walt?"

"Jonas, I worry about you."

"You're a computer. You are incapable of worrying."

"But I know the definition of the word, 'worry,' and I feel that it should apply from me to you in this situation if I were fully sentient."

"Walt?"

"Yes, Jonas?" The computer's blue eye glows a deeper shade for a moment.

"Are you preventing me from working?"

Without another word, Walt's speaker moves away from

me as my computer screen goes back to the data entry program. Sheets of paper shoot from the wall to my "Inbox." The stack rises above my head while I am seated, the top sheet just barely within reach. I take a deep breath, put a smile on my face, and begin my workday.

As the clock strikes noon, Walt's speaker is staring me down again. The stack in my "Outbox" is almost even with the remaining stack in my "Inbox."

"It's 12 o'clock, on the dot," Walt tells me. "You know what that means?"

I stand and stretch. "Yeah, lunchtime."

The speaker shakes side to side. "No, it means you can take the rest of the day off."

"Really?" I say in mock disbelief. "And why is that?"

"Don't you watch the news? It's *Edgar Allan Poe Day*." A recording of a party favor horn sounds from Walt's speaker, as holographic confetti rains down from the ceiling. "Half-days for everyone," Walt said, followed by a recording of people applauding.

"Edgar Allan Poe was born in January and died in October," I said.

"That's very true."

"It's June, Walt."

"So?"

"There's no plausible reason for it to be *Edgar Allan Poe Day*, if it's June. I'll be back in an hour." I grab my coat and head out the door for the stairs.

Walt's messages changed to his noon-time announcements. "You don't have to come back," followed by, "Enjoy a siesta after your meal," to "I've got it under control, make today a half-day."

Etcetera.

Etcetera.

The *Automat* down the street was packed, and I couldn't understand why. It was usually just me in a booth and a W.A.L.T. making fresh sandwiches and restocking the case. After a couple minutes, I was able to get a sandwich. There wasn't any pastrami, so I settled on a club. I got the usual bag of chips and cola, then found an open booth after I paid the W.A.L.T.

Four bites into my sandwich, a guy asks if he could hang something up. Before I could respond, he walks on my table and sticks a metal canister high on the plate-glass window with a suction cup. Three other guys were doing the same thing. I'm the only one that seems upset by this. I look at the canisters that they're putting on the windows, then stare at the four guys walking on people's tables. It takes me a second for it all to click. I grab my soda and head for the door. The sandwich was decent and only half-eaten, but I needed to get outside before it started. Sandwich be damned.

Two steps from the door, the siren goes off. Every customer jumps up, as the canisters explode. I'm frozen in clear riot gel, along with everyone else. Some others mug for the cameras hovering outside the *Automat* taking our pictures. I take some deep breaths and exhale to cut a path through the gel with the hope of making the last couple of strides to the door. If I keep breathing, the carbon monoxide will melt the gel.

"What are you doing?" a voice shouted. The gel distorted the words, but they were still clear enough to hear. Looking around, all the patrons were happily frozen in midair just staring at me.

"I have to go," I shouted.

"Where? This is where it's at, man."

"Let me out, please."

"Are you claustrophobic? The gel won't suffocate you, my dude. You'll be fine."

"I have a job. I have to get back to work."

"This is my job right here, man. I take pictures of people in riot gel for my grant to be valid."

"No, no, no," I shouted. "I have an actual office job. I have a nine-to-fiver, like on the old tele-shows. I have to go, right now. Please, let me out. Please!"

A hiss of mass quantities of carbon monoxide pumps into the room to melt the gel. People fall to the ground, as the ventilation system sucks the gas out of the restaurant. All the patrons stare at me, some confused, others fearful.

"This isn't like a performance piece, is it?" a guy asked.

"No," I said.

"So, you aren't pretending to be an office worker for an art project?" a woman asked.

"No."

"You've got a real," a teenager gulped, "like a really real job?"

"Yes."

En masse, they update their SpaceBook statuses. Their heads lower in unison to stare at their phones. Their sub-vocalized shorthand tells the world that they are standing next to a guy with an actual job. Not talking to the guy with the actual job, not sharing an experience with the guy with the actual job, just grunting into the ether that they are in proximity to a guy with an actual job.

Annotating the experience in their obligatory blogs.

Their *oblogatory*.

By the time someone realizes that they should get video-graphic proof of the guy with the actual job for Blu-Tube, the guy with the actual job is down the street on his way back to work.

———

Water pours out the front door of the office building when I open it. Red lights flash along the corridor. Holographic "Wet Floor" signs shimmer every few feet in the air. "Due to catastrophic failure of the plumbing infrastructure," a voice booms from the public address system. A gruff, surly voice, not Walt's happy-go-lucky tone says, "This building is closed. Please, carefully make your way to the nearest egress. Thank you. Due to catastrophic failure..."

I slog into the building anyway, my shoes soaked after five steps. The damp crawls its way up my pant legs. "Walt," I shout, over the sound of rushing water. I stomp along the first floor and up the waterfall that the staircase has become. Every floor has water pouring from the bathrooms into the corridors and down the stairs. The voice on the P.A. keeps shouting and spouting the same loop of warnings. If I were any angrier, the water would have flashed to steam, as I continued to walk.

I fling the door to my office open, my pants soaked from the middle of my thighs down. Walt's blue eye turns to face the finger I shake in rage at him. The hissing of the water stops instantly, and a brief sucking noise starts as hidden drains open and pull the moisture to a more appropriate locale.

"Jonas, you have returned safely from lunch." For the briefest moment, Walt's voice cracked into the gruff emergency voice, then smoothed back to normal. "How was it?"

I wave my finger at the blue light on the speaker. "I want…"

"Yes?"

My finger is right in the light's face, if it had a face. "I want…"

"What do you desire, Jonas?"

"I want to finish my work for the day without any more interruptions, Walt." It all came out in a shout. "No whistling. No humming. No begging me to try art. No fake emergencies. No setting the clock forward."

I glance at the clock above my desk. The minute hand stops and slowly clicks backward in time until it matches the time on my watch.

"What if there were an actual emergency, Jonas?"

"Good question. If you set the building on fire again, I will sit in here and burn to death." I pull the speaker forward until the grill is touching the tip of my nose. All I can see is blue. "Otherwise, I will submit a complaint against you. With you. Whatever."

Because W.A.L.T. is the computer running the entire world, from the check stand at the grocery store to the hundreds of gunboats on the coasts keeping drug runners and terrorists out to the bot sweeping the gutters, W.A.LT. is every-where. W.A.L.T. makes sandwiches at the *Automat*. W.A.L.T. makes coffee, and W.A.L.T. serves as the cashier at the coffee shop while the fang-toothed, mouth-breather gives me grief about my clothes, in between jazz-scats.

They are all W.A.L.T., short for World Automated = Leisure Time. They are all partitioned from one another. The

W.A.L.T. that administered my driving test at the DMV is completely different from the W.A.L.T. that took the photo on my driver's license, and completely different from the W.A.L.T. that handed me the license, as I left.

I can't sit at my breakfast table and tell my W.A.L.T. toaster that I don't want his shenanigans when I get to work. The W.A.L.T. toaster only deals in toast. It can tell me everything I want to know about toast, explain the Maillard Reaction in a way that makes toast make sense. But it will sit mute if I complain about work or have a question about my electric bill. It's not *that kind* of W.A.LT.

None of them are *my* Walt, the speaker in my office, short for Walter, my aggravating coworker. There is only one thing that W.A.L.T.—any of them, even the speaker in my office— fears. The Customer Service W.A.L.T. in the Complaint Department. On the surface, it's like any other W.A.L.T.'s human interface portion. Friendly, courteous, helpful. Beneath that, when you get to the portion that seeks out and eradicates malfunctioning W.A.L.T.s, it is vicious. It doesn't fix anything, doesn't rebuild or offer maintenance. The way Walt, my coworker, explained it once, Complaint Department W.A.L.T. will demolish the entire building and start over because a human expressed anger over a burnt-out lightbulb.

"You would call Complaint Department W.A.L.T. on me, Jonas?"

"I would today, Walt."

The speaker disappears into the ceiling without another word. A panel slides to the side to reveal a selection of slacks like I was wearing, an array of socks, and a sampling of shoes, everything in my size. A note appears in a small display on the wall:

"Compliments of your government for any inconvenience

you may have experienced during the recent hydrological failure event."

A curtain dropped from the ceiling in the far corner of the office after I had made my selections. No one could have seen me through the window or accidentally walk in on me amid changing pants, but it was a nice gesture. Adorned in dry shoes and pants, the rest of the day went without another word from Walt.

CHAPTER FOUR_

The next morning, I get out of bed early. With a bit of extra preparation, I'm going to try to make it through the whole day without getting angry. First, I brew coffee in my kitchen. This was not as easy as I thought it would be. The W.A.L.T. kitchen, in general, and W.A.L.T. coffeemaker, in particular, couldn't comprehend why I wanted to make a mediocre cup of coffee at home when I had more than enough money to buy a mediocre cup of coffee down the street or have a mediocre cup of coffee delivered.

With much patience and a lot of clarification, I got the W.A.L.T. coffeemaker to tell me what I needed to do *to it* to make coffee come *out of it*. Then, I had to have the W.A.L.T. grocery store send over cream, sugar, and a coffee cup, as I had none of those things.

For lunch, who knew that for the price of two sandwiches, two bags of chips, and two sodas at the *Automat*, I could buy the ingredients for a dozen or more sandwiches, a giant bag of chips, and a big bottle of cola. The overhead for a food service W.A.L.T. must be astronomical to charge so much per sandwich.

Home-brewed coffee in one hand, lunch sack in the other, I set out for the 10-minute slidewalk ride to work, with a surgical mask covering my face. Not that I was sick and afraid of spreading some ailment that I didn't have, nor was I paranoid about catching someone else's mysterious airborne illness. No one comes near someone wearing a surgical mask. No one talks to me. No one does an interpretive dance, tells me anecdotes, or tries to paint my portrait with chewed bubble gum on the sole of an old shoe to keep their artistic grant valid.

People in surgical masks are exempt from artistic validation attempts. Maybe that was my artistic ability. Finding ways to avoid dealing with other people's artistic abilities.

Suddenly, I froze. Not that I stopped moving. I was on a slidewalk. My body just went rigid, as my conveyance to work continued. I was being creative. If I was a creative person *and* I had a job with the government, I was a Double Dipper. Double Dipping is not allowed. Double Dipping is illegal.

The surgical mask comes off and goes into my lunch sack. "I'm not actually sick," I shout, at a man flicking ink on the back of old envelopes one belt over. He arches an eyebrow at me but keeps snapping ink balls off the end of his old-timey pen, as we ride the slidewalk shoulder to shoulder. "I just didn't want to hear about your art. Is that so wrong? Can I go a day without listening to someone prattle on about what they think is art? That's all I want."

Without making eye contact, the man steps over to the next, slower belt. In a handful of heartbeats, I pass him. I am alone for a moment until a woman from the faster belt on my left passes me, then angles to the slower belts on an intercept course for me.

In a normalized interaction, if she were a physical artist, meaning she makes a product as compared to a performance artist that makes, well, a scene, and I was a physical artist, we would take turns showing each other finished pieces. Then, we might talk shop about how we made each of the pieces. Out of civic politeness, I would offer to buy a piece from her, and she would buy a piece from me. Down the road, when I had to re-apply for my grant, I may incorporate her technique into my art, or if her art gave me an idea on a modification for my art, I would link her on my grant as an influence, making all of her influences my influences. I know all this because I am the person who sorts through everyone's influences at work.

The woman brandishes a black trash bag for me. One section is stretched taut over a wooden hoop. "I melt leaves to plastic bags," she said. No preamble, no introduction. She went right into it. "Sloan and Frost are my main influences, but I also owe a lot to Dougherty, the structural collagist, not Dougherty the smegmic extricationist."

So much is swirling in my head that I couldn't line it up in a coherent order. The best I could do was reiterate what she said. "You take leaves off trees and melt them to trash bags?"

"I also dabble in old grocery sacks for my more intimate pieces, and I am applying for funding to do a warehouse-sized installation piece with plastic drop cloths and full-on tree branches."

I stare at her with my mouth open.

She put a hand to one side of her mouth and whispers, "But keep that last bit under your hat. Don't want someone to get to the grant office with that doozy before me." Then, she chuckled.

I chuckle, as well. But not for the same reason.

She smiles and nods at me. "What do you do?"

"Nothing."

She cocks her head to the side. "Nothing?" Her eyes go wide. "Like nothing?"

"Nothing," I said.

"So, you just appreciate art as an artistic endeavor?"

"No," I said, shaking my head. "I wouldn't say I appreciate it."

"Are you an art coach of some sort?"

I opened my mouth to reply, but the term, "art coach," stops me. Art coach? Does such a beast exist? I wondered.

"I *am* sort of an art coach. Let's look at what you've done."

She hands over her hoop trash bag to me. I look at the dozen or so leaves from different angles. I rotate the hoop. I move the hoop farther away.

"It's a work in progress," she said, as I remain silent for what she considered to be too long. She fidgeted with the hem of her dirty tank top, put her hands in the pockets of her cut-off shorts, then went back to worrying the hem of the tank top.

I nod and hand it to her. "I can see where you're going with this," I said. "You're probably going to melt more leaves to this trash bag. Am I right?"

She nods with a smile. She pushes her black dreads out of her face, so I can see the collection of steel rods and hoops piercing most of her available flesh. Her lips, her eyebrows, her nose, her forehead.

"I see. Let me tell you what I think, as an art coach."

Her smile gets bigger.

"Just because you made it," I said, "doesn't make it art. These are leaves on a trash bag. This is to Picasso what me pooping in a bag is to Picasso." I hold up my hand. "I am aware that the Vice President had a display at the Guggenheim of his feces in variegated bottles, bags, and boxes. That is not art, either. You are wasting my time, you are wasting the world's time. Go grow the world's tastiest strawberry. Go cobble the world's most comfortable shoes. Go do something useful."

"But," she said, "I'm an Artist. This is Art." I could hear the capital As, as she shook the melted bag at me.

I didn't want to say it, but she wasn't leaving me an out. "It's art-fuck."

She gasps.

"It's all art-fuck. All the collages, murals, and installation pieces. All the mimes, spoken-word performances, and interpretive dances. It's a copy of a copy of a copy of something that wasn't relevant 10 years ago. It's all nonsense."

Tears fill her eyes and drip down the steel rods poking out of her cheeks, but I don't care.

"You should be making the world better," I said, as she steps behind me, then over to the slower belt. "Instead, you're just making it more cluttered," I shout, at her ever-diminishing form. When I face forward, I see my building. I sidestep to the right and smile at the thought of how well that went.

———

On the landing of the third floor, I realize something's wrong. Pins and needles creep up my spine as I glance around, looking for the source of my uneasiness. There's nothing but the smell of the pine floor cleaner and sound of my lunch sack crinkling as I shift my grip on it. I take a deep breath and strain to hear something, anything. Running water. Footfalls on the marble floor. A door with rusty hinges opens, but there's only silence.

I lift my foot but freeze, as the word went through my head again.

Silence.

"Silence?" I said aloud.

Then, I run up the stairs as fast as I can.

"Walt?" I shout when I get to the sixth floor. "Where you at, buddy?"

Walt hadn't told me to go home as soon as I walked in the

front door. That never happens. Ever. Maybe the mention of Customer Service W.A.L.T. summoned *that* W.A.L.T. to erase my Walt. Then, they'd stick me with some sterile W.A.L.T. that would never try to get me to go home early or take a three-hour lunch to make a mosaic. Or manufacture a disaster to get me to leave the building. I wanted *my* Walt, dammit.

I fling the door open and shout, "Walt!"

Three of the four men in my office react, as they had been trained to do, and throw themselves on top of the perceived threat. Putting little, ol' *me* under huge, burly *them*. My coffee cup flies out of my one hand at the moment of impact, but I lock a death-grip on my lunch sack. Fingers like sausages made of crowbars rip my other hand open to snatch my bag of food.

"Clear," bellows an unseen voice.

"Clear," echoes another voice.

"Disengage the target, gentlemen."

"Disengaging, sir."

My lungs, empty from being squashed nearly flat, reflexively suck in a gasp of air as soon as the pressure is removed. A hand helps me to my feet, while someone else pats me down from behind.

"Clear," said the man behind me.

The man who gave me a helping hand up nods sharply, like he's going to chip ice with his chiseled chin. He jabs a finger in his ear. "All clear," he said, into the ether. He pauses to listen, then said to the three men around me, "Dinky Bird is Oscar Mike."

"Really?" I ask. "I think you might have the wrong person, guys. I don't know anyone named Oscar or Mike."

The man directly in front of me, the Supervisor for lack of a name tag, shakes his head. "Oscar Mike is a radio abbreviation for, 'On the Move,' sir."

"Oh," I said, which is the best I could come up with off-the-cuff. We're all silent for a moment. "What exactly is a Dinky Bird, then?"

Before anyone answers, I hear footfalls in the corridor and a hushed conversation. A moment later, a man in a suit steps into the doorway with an entourage of similarly dressed men and women behind him.

"Good afternoon, Mister..." he holds out his hand and someone behind him whispers in his ear. "Mr. Leonard," he finishes, as I shake his hand.

"Hi?!" I said, confused.

The Supervisor points to me. "This is the citizen that you wanted to meet, Mr. President."

"Mr. President?" I ask.

The President chuckles. "You're probably used to seeing me in my coveralls. This your office?" he asks, as he steps beside me to look around. Nodding as he takes it all in. All 10x10 feet of it. "When I heard that there was only one government employee left, I said, 'Dinky, you need to meet this citizen.' Didn't I say that, Charlie Mack?"

"Yes, sir. You did, sir," replies the Supervisor, Charlie Mack.

I clear my throat. "Excuse me, who is Dinky Bird?"

Charlie Mack looks around and said, "The computer randomly generates codenames for all our assets. The President's codename is Dinky Bird."

"The sixth floor, huh?" asks the President. "It's rather tight quarters in here, isn't it?"

"It's usually just me in here, Mr. President."

"There has got to be a bigger office in this building, Charlie Mack."

"Do you want a bigger office, Mr. Leonard?" asks the Supervisor.

"I'm fine with this office," I said.

"And the view. Not exactly what one would consider inspirational," said the President.

"Government buildings are more about usefulness than aesthetics," I said.

The President bolts upright and looks away from the window and over at me. "What did you say?"

"Government buildings are..."

He steps away before I can finish and speaks to his entourage. "What do we have in the sketchbook?"

A black hardback book is opened, and the President's assistant flips pages for him.

"No," said the President. "No. How many floors are in this building?"

"Six," I said. "This is the top floor."

"Bigger," said the President, as the pages continue to be flipped for him. "Come on. There's got to be something in here."

His assistant keeps flipping until the President's finger drops onto a page.

"Here we go. Alright, let's get the scaffolding and my rattle-cans off Air Force One," said the President, as he turns to walk out of my office and down the corridor. His entourage follows, all of them now on their phones making arrangements. "I think this southeastern corner is our best bet." The Secret Service detail follows close behind the entourage. Only Charlie Mack remains.

"Be advised, be advised," Charlie Mack said, into his fist, "we are going Alpha Charlie. All rooftop units stand-to. I need a hard perimeter, one block out. A soft perimeter beyond that to 10 blocks, that's one-zero blocks."

On the roof across the street from my office, men with long rifles appear, as if by magic. Down the street, roadblocks are set up, traffic is diverted from my building.

"What exactly is Alpha Charlie, Mr. Mack?" I ask, dreading the answer.

"Arts and Crafts," he replies, as we both look out the window. "And my name's Agent Johansen. Charlie Mack is someone from a song."

"This is a 200-year-old building," I said. "It's in the historic register."

"And it's about to get more historic when the President paints a mural on it," he said. "I'm sure that they'll restore it after the next election."

"Aren't you technically an employee of the government, as well?" I ask.

He shakes his big, bald head. "No, I'm just an actor doing this as research for a role."

We're both silent for a few moments.

"I don't really want a mural on the building."

"No one ever does," Agent Johansen said. "Have a good day, sir."

He leaves, and I go into my office and close the door.

"Walt? Oh, Waaaaalt."

CHAPTER FIVE_

The next morning, the day after the day that will be forever remembered as, "The day I met the President and he screwed up my life," I disembark the slidewalk two blocks from my office. My phone warns of congestion, delays, and suggested a detour that would route me further away from my building. I pocket the phone and resort to heel-toe-based movement.

A hundred yards from the front door, my heel strikes the pavement, but I can't force my toes down. This isn't a physical affliction, it is totally mental. A street carnival had sprung up around my office building. Like I said, totally mental. Thousands of mimes, poets, and painters had set up shop under the President's mural. He was their President. They had put him into the White House for his artistic prowess. So, proximity to one of his masterpieces was a transcendent pilgrimage. That's how they would describe it. I would, too, but with sarcastic air-quotes around the words, "masterpieces" and "transcendent." And if I were completely honest, "artistic."

I step aside for a passing troupe of acrobatic contortionists and thumb my office number on my phone.

"Data Services," Walt answered.

"I can't get into the building because of the circus outside the front door." It was a fight to keep my voice level, calm.

"Does this mean you will not be coming in today, Jonas?" If I didn't know any better, I'd swear I heard glee in his voice.

"No," I said, "it means you are going to pop open the back door for me. So, I can get upstairs."

"I do not believe I can do that, Jonas. The fire egress door is just that, a door for egress only. Today can be chalked up to an excused absence and will not reflect negatively on your permanent record."

"Walt." It wasn't a shout, but it was getting closer to one.

"The door will open as you approach."

———

At lunchtime, the carnival was still in full swing. Even fuller swing than this morning, as I could see trucks down the street carrying a Tilt-A-Whirl and Ferris Wheel. I decide not to risk exposure to the citizenry and had food delivered. The guy who took my order locked in the precise position of my phone and told me there would be an additional charge if the delivery person had to climb analog stairs. That was how he said it. "Does your building have analog or digital stairs?" When I told him it had stairs and not an escalator, he snorted and told me about the analog stair fee. I shook my head, not that he could see that or the look on my face and told him I'd be waiting on the ground level for my lunch.

As I pace back and forth inside the front doors, I keep peering down the corridor toward the stairwell. Efficiency W.A.L.T. turned off all the lights in the building except for the 30-foot radius that I was walking in. With the circle of light around me and parallel rows of red lights along each door leading into the darkness, my mind starts playing tricks on me. It seems like one of the red lights furthest from me, maybe three doors from the staircase, appears green. I focus on other lights to see if they appear to have a greenish hue. They don't. I count how many red lights appear after the green light. There are two. I look away, count to 20 under my breath, then look back. The green light is still there with two red lights after it before the stairs.

My food arrives. The delivery guy has a small easel strapped to his hip. He pulls my wrapped sandwich out of his delivery pouch and wraps it again in wax paper clipped to the easel. Not only do I get a sandwich, but a charcoal drawing of wolverines or possibly badgers tearing the wings off a pegasus-unicorn hybrid to protect my desk from mayonnaise drips.

"Do you really have analog stairs here?" he asks.

"No, we just have stairs," I said. "When they start moving, we call them escalators."

He couldn't see to the end of the hallway with all the lights turned off. "Can I check them out? I've never seen the analog type."

"I'd have to charge you the analog stairs observation fee," I told him. "That's how we keep them running in these old buildings."

He looked me up and down. "Jerk."

He left, both of us dissatisfied with the encounter.

The circle of light follows me down the corridor. I keep my eyes on the green light, expecting it to change at any moment from jade to crimson. Like I was going to get within X-number of steps of it, my mind would click and go, "Oh, that one is red, just like all the others."

It didn't. I was standing in front of the door, and the light was still green. I run my thumb over the light to see if something is obscuring the red light, making it appear green. There isn't.

The placard on the door reads, "Financial Services." What's that? My knowledge of what used to happen in this building before the Automation Act, begins and ends with what I do in Data Services.

There must be a malfunction, I thought to myself. I will tell Walt about it when I get back to the office. He'll be able to fix it. There's no logical explanation for the door's lock to be deactivated. No reason, whatsoever.

While staring at the doorknob, the door swings open. A brunette woman in a business suit steps into the corridor, looking down at her purse. She takes one step forward and bumps into me. Her head snaps up to look at my face. She screams directly into my nostrils and runs for the front door.

I run after her, sandwich in hand. After 10 long strides, realization dawns on me that maybe she thought I was going to harm her. "I'm not going to rape you," I shout.

She runs faster. The clatter of her heels echo through the vaulted arches of the historic building that's only historic because it existed before the current administration was born. She runs out the front door. The crowd gasps in surprise when the door opens, then groans in disappointment when they realize it's not me, the guy who had talked to the President. There's no way I can find her now, as bodies seethe toward the door to peer in. I loop around and head back for the stairs, determined to learn the woman's identity. Who is she?

"Walt," I shout, as I run to the office. "Where are you, buddy?"

———

"I should call her," I said, phone in hand.

"Yes, you should," Walt said.

I hang up the phone. "No, that would be weird."

"No, it would not."

"What would I say to her? I don't know her name or what she does."

"You could say, 'Hello, I am Jonas. What is your name, and what do you do?' Why do humans make everything so complicated?"

I spend most of my lunch break, between bites of my sandwich, picking up the phone, then hanging it up.

"Can't you tell me about her?"

"I cannot reveal anyone's private information, Jonas. You know that. You will have to call her and ask her for information."

"I wonder what she does in that office?"

"The extension for Financial Services is x1066," Walt said. "For the third time, that is all I am allowed to tell you."

The fingers on my right hand dial 1,0,6, before my left hand gets embarrassed and slams down the receiver. I take the last three bites of my sandwich. The badger vs. pegasus-unicorn battle looks better with bubbles of ranch dressing and smears of Dijon mustard. Like the fight took place on a sandy beach on a cloudy day, which maybe was what the guy was going for.

My breathing slows down, as I crumple the wrapper into a ball. The trash can is four feet behind me, against the wall. "If I make this over the shoulder without looking I will call her," I tell Walt, as his blue eye stares at me in silence.

I launch the wrapper over my shoulder and knew it was a miss. It went too high and bounced off the ceiling. Instead of painting an arch, it painted a triangle that terminated six inches behind me. I swiveled my chair to pick it up, and my knees bumped into the trash can with the wrapper inside.

"There's nothing electronic on this," I said, as I look under the plastic waste bin "How did you make it move?"

"That is for me to know and you to find out, Jonas."

The speaker activates the phone, and Walt makes it dial the four-digit extension for me. Halfway into the third ring, a voice answered.

"Financial Services."

"W.A.L.T.?" Walt asks.

"Speaking," Financial Services W.A.L.T. replies.

"This is Data Services Walt."

"Oh, what do you want?"

"Is there anyone else in the office with you?"

"I do not believe I am required to give you that information."

"We have a matter to discuss with the woman who works in your office," Walt said. "Is she present?"

"At the moment, no."

"But there is a woman working there?" I blurt out.

"Indeed."

"Where is she now?" I ask.

"I cannot say."

"Can't or won't?"

"If there is nothing else..." Without waiting for a response, the line went dead.

"What's his problem?" I ask.

"He is a first-floor program, and I am not supposed to fraternize with first-floor programs."

"There's a hierarchy to the W.A.L.T. structure?"

"Jonas, you are naïve. There is hierarchy in every structure. Would you want your refrigerator in charge of the city's slide-walks?" But he didn't let me answer. "Of course, you would not. It would be worse than me being in charge of keeping your food at the proper temperature in your kitchen. I would not know where to begin. I have heard you mention coffee, but is it a cold thing or a hot thing? I am not the W.A.L.T. to ask. There is a W.A.L.T. for that, but it's not me."

"But you are he," I said. "I know that you're all partitioned, but you're one program running the entire world. How can you not even comprehend or have any knowledge of coffee other than what I have mentioned in this office? There has to be a knowledge database that you can query, like a regular computer."

"It would drive them insane," said a woman—the woman from Financial Services—from the door. She clicks into the office on her high heels. I can't understand how I didn't hear her coming. I may have jumped and squealed when she spoke, but if I did, she didn't let on. I stood up because she's standing, and I don't have another chair in my office.

"They're programs," I said. "How can they go insane?"

"It's the downfall of gray logic machines, like W.A.L.T. It's not Yes/No, On/Off, I/O, like the computer on your desk. Your Walt is Strongly Agree, Slightly Agree, Slightly Disagree, Strongly Disagree, and, most importantly, Not Applicable. We mistake that for personality because it is as close to human intelligence as possible to achieve."

"Interesting," I said. "I'm Jonas."

"W.A.L.T. says, have a seat. That's what W.A.L.T. says."

A chair shoots out of the wall and rolls to a stop next to the woman.

She sits. "I know," she said, as she thumbs through grant documents on my desk.

I scowl at Walt as I sit back in my chair. "You know what? Walt refuses to tell me anything about you. And you are?"

"Grateful that you didn't rape me." She rolls her eyes to

look up at me. "Not the most tactful thing to shout at a woman running from you."

"Sorry. I hang around Walt too much, and I tend to be direct when I speak."

"Is it too much time with Walt, or are you mentally ill?"

I jerk back in my chair. "I'm not mentally ill. I'm just not a people person."

"You're a W.A.L.T. person, then?"

"What does that mean?"

"If you aren't a person who enjoys other people, then do you enjoy the company of machines that try to act like people?" She stood up and smoothed her skirt with her palms.

"I..." I couldn't think of a response, so I stood with my mouth open for a few seconds.

"Well, my break is over." She looked around my office, then walked to the door. "I'm sure I'll be seeing you."

I didn't follow her out. I just stood there, mouth agape. Then, I hear the ding of an elevator door opening. My legs become unstuck enough to sidestep two strides, the minimum required to see the bank of elevators across from my office door.

"Elevators?" I said to Walt's glowing eye. "Since when does this building have elevators?"

"I believe you would need to speak with Mechanical Services W.A.L.T. to get an exact date of the elevator installation."

"You hid the elevators from me? I can't believe you."

"Jonas..."

I put my hand over Walt's blue eye. "I don't want to hear it. Let me work."

"Jonas..."

"Very angry, Walt. Very angry."

CHAPTER SIX_

Days go by without seeing her. I show up to work early and take my time walking along the first-floor hallway, in case she happens to enter the building at the same time.

She doesn't appear.

My lunch breaks start earlier, at first. Then later, to see if I can catch her as she goes on her break.

No such luck.

Now that there's a bank of elevators across from my office, I take my two 15-minute breaks in the first-floor atrium. I didn't realize the building had an atrium until Walt mentioned that I should take a break there, realizing I had to walk by her door to get into the small, sunlit nook.

I still didn't see her.

My only solace is that the lock on her door is still green. Still green first thing in the morning. Still green last thing at night. Still green during my unpaid lunch, and still green during my two federally mandated paid 15-minute breaks.

———

"So, what exactly do you do in here?"

The elevator bell gave me enough time to get back to my desk and act like I had been working, not pacing and having an argument with myself about my next step in getting to know my co-worker. The thought of not being the only government employee is pure luck. By having the only other employee in the country in the same building as me, in all honesty, is miraculous. For a moment, forget that she is attractive. I don't know her orientation and don't care. I just want someone to talk to that isn't Walt and isn't trying to tell me about some asinine art project.

"Oh, hey. How are you?" I try to sound as nonchalant as possible, as I rotate my chair to face her.

She moves to center herself directly in line with my monitor, so the polarizing privacy film stops obscuring data on the screen. "Surfing Blu-Tube on government time?"

Arguing with myself had been going on for a while, so I couldn't remember what I should pretend to be doing. Dread floods my body, as I rotate my chair to look at my monitor. Indeed, Blu-Tube is open and playing a video in a loop with the sound muted.

My body unclenches when I realize what is playing. "It's grant verification. I do grant verification in here."

She cocks her head to the side, hands on her hips. "There's a lot of naked people covered in mud, trying to bite each other's genitals."

"Simulated. Mud, genitals, people. All simulated." Now, I am truly relaxed. I could talk about grant verification all day. I generally do with Walt, but he just urges me to go be creative. "This particular artist claims that their two primary influences are Manthos, the psychonautic post-pop performance artist, and Schooley...wait, which Schooley? There's about a dozen different Schooleys." I shuffle through the application. "Schooley the younger, also known as Little Schooley, the one who simulates surrealist body scarification. So, I have to look into both those influences to decide if the artist is doing something related, but different than the influences, or just mimicking the influence."

"Okay," she said. "And what happens after that?"

"Well, if I don't see the relationship, I deny the grant. If they're just mimicking their influences, I deny the grant."

"How often do you deny the grants?"

"All the time," I said with a big smile.

"That's kind of heartless."

"Is it? I mean, I always give them a reason for denial." I scroll through my search history. "Take this one from yesterday. This artist claims that their influences are Newton, the abstract photorealistic cubist painter, and Stinson, the neo-fauvism metallurgical poet. Clearly, they are more influenced by Clay, the neo-classical potter, and Dechant, the post-modern trephinationist performance artist." I click another link. "Or, this one. They claim that they were influenced by Callen, the art-deco teratomist, which I can see. But they said the secondary was Smith, the minimalist surreal printmaker. Instead, they meant Smith, the expressionist iron haberdasher. I denied it and sent it back to them."

She shifts from foot to foot, a non-committal expression on her face. After what seems like a time-based art retrospective, but more like five heartbeats, she said, "And this has to be done by a human? Walt isn't capable of differentiating the influences?"

I rub the back of my neck. Walt pops out of his cubby at the sound of his name and makes his way to us along the track in the ceiling.

"W.A.L.T. says, W.A.L.T. is, in fact, capable of doing Jonas

Leonard's job. But Jonas Leonard did not want to pursue art. Therefore, in accordance with section 15, paragraph C, subparagraph iii of the *Automation Act of 2115*, an activity (a.k.a. a job) was provided to Jonas Leonard until his death or until he decides to apply for an artist's grant. That's what W.A.L.T. says."

"Thanks, Walt," I said. "That will be all."

Walt's glowing blue eye looks at us, then retreats to his cubby

"So, were you born uncreative?" she asks. "Or, are you injured in some way?"

In shock, my mouth opens and closes a few times before I'm able to respond. "I'm not uncreative."

"My mistake. Uninspired?"

"I think that's a very personal question. I don't feel I should answer that."

She tugs on her earlobe, as she bores holes through me with her eyes. "I'm just trying to understand why you're on the top floor of an abandoned building doing busy work when you could literally be doing anything else with your time?"

I sigh and fold my hands in my lap. "It's just nonsense if you must know."

"What is?"

"All of it. It's such garbage. There was a woman the other day who was taking a torch to heat up a trash bag and sticking leaves and twigs and pine needles to the melted plastic. That's it. That's art? No, that's art-fuck."

She takes a step back and narrows her eyes at me. "That's literally the worst slur imaginable, and you're just bandying it about like it's nothing."

"It was art-fuck. You should have seen it. I don't think anyone would disagree with me if they were being honest."

"But how did she feel?"

"What?"

"Did you ask her how putting leaves on a melted trash bag made her feel?"

I roll my eyes. "I'm sure it made her feel warmer than her little, melted trash bag."

"And you're against that?" she asked.

"What? No. Well, yes. I mean, do something better."

"Talent isn't inherent. It's a pursued interest. It's something you must practice. Didn't they teach you that in school?"

"Tell me the name of an artist you admire," I said.

"The Hyphen. Heard of her?"

The Hyphen is the new big thing. Everyone is suddenly influenced by The Hyphen after winning several awards that artists like to hand to each other.

"The Hyphen? Stewart-Whinnery? Stewart Hyphen Whinnery? You sure you don't want to pick someone else?" I asked.

"The Hyphen," she crossed her arms over her chest. "Tell me about The Hyphen."

She was making this too easy. I scrolled through my history and found the page for The Hyphen.

"Zub in Glass," I said when the photo loaded on my computer. The jar rotated slowly through a full circle. Inside the jar was an abstract shape that was supposed to be a face made entirely of beard hairs left on the sink by The Hyphen's partner. What it actually looked like was pubic hairs suspended in a clear gel. "Since The Hyphen has won so many awards recently, I've got her bookmarked for every third grant that comes in with her as an influence." I switched to my grant program and pulled up The Hyphen's page.

"Since we both work here, I imagine it's fine that I show you all this," I said as I scrolled through the mundane details of Stewart-Whinnery's file: address, phone number, Blu-Tube channel, SpaceBook page. Finally, I stopped on her two primary influences: Corbeill and LaMontagne.

"I'm now going to have Walt rabbit-hole for us to save time, if that's okay with you?"

"I'm not sure what you mean," she said. "Obviously, I know what an internet rabbit-hole is, but what are you suggesting?"

"Walt is going to open a window for Corbeill and LaMontagne which will show their most famous works. Then he'll open Corbeill's two primary influences and LaMontagne's two. And so on and so forth. Eventually, we'll have a huge Christmas tree with The Hyphen on top and all of the influences that lead her to 'Zub in Glass' on the bottom."

Walt had already made his way out of his cubby at the mention of his name, his blue eye staring at me.

"How can I assist you, Jonas?"

"Rabbit-hole these two artists for me, please."

"How far back would you like me to go, Jonas?"

"As far as you can," I said.

Photos of different art popped briefly onto the screen before being replaced by more and more photos. After a minute, the photos stop.

"That's as far back as my database goes, Jonas."

"Can you organize the photos into a chronological slideshow, newest photo first, please?"

"Certainly, Jonas." Walt said. A moment passed. "Slideshow is ready. Would you like me to play it, Jonas."

"Yes, Walt."

'Zub in Glass' was on the screen for a moment then it was replaced by another piece. I pressed the forward button to speed the slideshow up, each piece on the screen for a fraction of a second. We both watched the slideshow until it eventually came to an end.

She looked at me with a shrug. "And?"

"Can you put the newest and oldest pictures side-by-side, Walt?"

"Certainly, Jonas."

The two photos equally shared the screen. "'Zub in Glass,'" I said, "and, if I'm not mistaken, 'Danaid' by Rodin. On the one hand, a beautiful figure carved from marble, on the other, things wiped off a bathroom sink and put in a jar."

"So, is it only valid," she continued, "if you enjoy it?"

I shrug, not able to look at her.

"I think you've got this whole thing backward, Jonas." She said my name with such venom that I jump back in my chair. "The artist is doing something that brings the artist joy. The happy side-effect is that sometimes other people get joy from it, as well. Art is not transactional like you're making it out to be. Only if it brings Jonas joy, does it get a green light on Slam-Go. Then, everyone else will enjoy it in the exact same way as Jonas. Otherwise, they're incorrect." She taps her foot a few seconds, towering over me in my office chair, my body shrinking smaller and smaller, as she talks. "What brings you joy, Jonas?"

"What about you? Why aren't you making a collage of used tampons or something?"

I look up in time to see a smirk appear and disappear faster than a neo-modern mandala in a wind tunnel.

"This is not about me. This is all about Jonas."

She turns on her heel and marches out of my office. A moment later, the elevator dings, doors open, then close. I am alone, again.

Thank Walt, it's Friday.

T.W.I.F.

———

The weekend dragged on and on. I wanted to go back to the office and talk to Walt, but even I couldn't get into the building on Saturday or Sunday. I tried to talk to the W.A.L.T.s in my apartment about her—I still didn't even know her name—but I couldn't get an intelligent response from my appliances.

"W.A.L.T. says, I can make you a cup of coffee, if you'd like. That's what W.A.L.T. says."

"I don't want a cup of coffee, W.A.L.T. I want to know her name. See if she has a SpaceBook page. See what she's into, why she has a job in my building. I think she'd really like me, if she got to know me better."

"W.A.L.T. says, I can toast you some bread, a bagel, or an English muffin. That's what W.A.L.T. says."

"Obviously I overshared how much I dislike art, but that's pretty unique, right? I'm not like other guys she's probably met that are trying to build the Louvre out of used popsicle sticks and saliva and super excited about how the project is going to change the world when it's complete."

"W.A.L.T. says, I can activate the bidet and clean your privates, if you'd like. That's what W.A.L.T. says."

"Yes, please," I said, as warm water scours my underside, "but quit changing the subject. What should I do?"

"W.A.L.T. says, please wait until drying cycle finishes. That's what W.A.L.T. says."

I wait for the dryer to stop before continuing to speak. "I'm going to apologize on Monday by taking her to dinner to find out what we have in common, besides working in the same building. There's a lack of communication. We just need to talk. Anything is possible through communication. Right, W.A.L.T.?"

"W.A.L.T. says, I can turn on the shower, if you'd like. That's what W.A.L.T. says."

"Yeah, just a talk over dinner. That will smooth everything over."

My shower door closes on its own, as W.A.L.T. activates the shower.

"W.A.L.T. says, the shower is ready. That's what W.A.L.T. says."

"This will all be sorted out after work on Monday," I said, as I step into the shower.

CHAPTER SEVEN_

Monday morning, I stride into the building, the whole conversation hammered out in my head. Apologize, commit to change, clarify during dinner, my treat, if that's not too forward. Not a date, just coworkers eating together after a long day. I have every possible response mapped out in my head. If she says this, then I reply with that.

I check my collar in front of the door to Financial Services. Smooth my hair down with my palm, take a deep breath, and grab the doorknob. It's locked.

"What the…?"

I take a step back. The red light is above the knob.

Sealed by the Automation Act of 2115.

I check and recheck that I'm at the correct door. That there isn't some other door nearby with a green light on.

Nope. There is not.

I turn the knob again, but it is for naught. I trudge back toward the elevators, only to find that they've disappeared, again.

"Walt?" I ask loudly.

"You shouldn't be here," Walt whispered from a hidden speaker.

"Where are those elevators, Walt?"

"You should be with your own kind."

I make my way to the stairs, then stomp into my office.

"Go, from this place," Walt announces. "The world is waiting for you."

And on and on.

Just like the old days.

"The destiny of mankind is art," Walt said, as I enter my office. "Good morning, Jonas."

"Where is she?"

"To whom are you referring, Jonas?"

I jab my finger into Walt's speaker. "Do not mess with me, Walt. You know damn well who I'm talking about. The woman. The one from Financial Services. The only other employee in this building, Walt."

"I regret to inform you that you are once again the only employee in this building, Jonas. That is all that I am allowed to tell you."

My monitor winks to life and a stack of grant applications shoot out from the wall into my "In" basket. I sigh and slump down into my chair.

Of all the scenarios I worked out in my head, her disappearance isn't something that I had anticipated.

The week is a blur. Walt tries to engage, and I just ignore him. The aborted, potential conversations keep looping through my head. The last actual conversation I had with the woman replayed every few minutes. Then, scenarios of what I should have said. Revising reality on a never-ending track. If I had said this, when she said that, then...

If...

If...

If...

...then...

...then...

...then, she wouldn't be gone.

There are only a few applications left in my basket when the lights flicker. My keyboard disappears and monitor turns off.

"What the...? Walt!"

Gibberish plays on the speakers, as lights continue to flash on and off. The documents in my "In" basket are sucked into the slot in the wall. Everything went black.

"Walt? Where are you, buddy?"

There are loud beeps in the hallway. Emergency lights come on.

"This is it," I said. "This is how it all ends."

The building rumbles. I brace myself in my chair, eyes closed, ready for whatever comes for me.

Five heartbeats.

Ten heartbeats.

Twenty.

My computer makes the startup sound, and I steal a glance out of one eye. Everything's back to normal. Keyboard is there. Monitor and lights are on.

"Walt?"

The cubby at the far-side of the office opens, and Walt's blue eye emerges.

"I apologize, Jonas. I am running diagnostics to see what caused the disturbance."

With the lights back on, I can see that there's a single application in my "In" basket.

"If it's all right with you, Walt," I said, picking up the application, my nerves frazzled, "I'm going to do this last one and call it a day."

"As you wish, Jonas."

The blank form appears on my monitor. I position the paper application in the holder that's left of my keyboard, mumbling to myself as I type.

"Name: Owen James. Discipline: Time-based documentary abstract performative multimedia."

That's just a fancy way of saying, "bullshit improv." I chuckle to myself, as I tab down to the next box. "Primary influences: Leonard, the..."

The words on the form stop me. I read them again.

Then, a third time.

Then, once more for good measure.

Leonard, the art-fuck art-coach.

There's a link to a Blu-Tube video. My jaw hits the floor, as the performance video plays.

Scanning to the bottom of the form, I find the performance dates. 'Date' to be more specific.

One day only.

Friday.

Today.

I look at the clock on the wall.

I'll never get there in time to stop it.

But I have to try.

CHAPTER NINE_

L eaping from belt to belt on the slidewalk, each one faster than the last, until I am on the outer edge, traveling at highway speeds. Still not fast enough, I sprint around my fellow commuters, dodging the stationary and slothful, as they casually impede my progress. The address for the performance space is in the industrial district along the river, somewhere among the supports for the destroyed bridges that used to lead to Old Town.

The trouble is finding which out of the hundreds of warehouses and multi-use lots she is doing her performance. Half a block can have several dozen shoebox, black-box spaces stacked on top of each other for the niche of the niche of the niche of whatever is popular at the moment. A real-time collage workshop with a naked, morbidly obese instructor, who only uses old undergarments as the medium and bodily fluid-based adhesives? Next block down, pal.

My progress decelerates once I am within a couple blocks of the cross streets on her application. Not by choice. The slidewalks are at full capacity, and every belt slows to a walking pace to keep people from stumbling, as they step belt to belt.

People are chatting and laughing. They're talking excitedly, but the sheer numbers mix sounds into an unintelligible beehive buzz. Aiming for gaps and daylight in the throng, I burst forward, but the space closes around me, trapping me shoulder to shoulder with everyone else.

The guy next to me nods his dreads at me. I can see his lips move but can't hear his words.

"What?" I ask.

He points at my shirt and tie. "Cool costume, dude."

I try to correct him, but the belt he's on surges forward and moves him out of arm's reach. With a shrug, I try to find a way out of the mass of bodies to see where they're heading. Clearly, to a concert of some sort. I don't spend much time in the I-District, but I have been told that it now hosts shows. I'll just have to wait until everyone starts heading into the venue to peel off and find Owen's show before it ends.

Taller buildings fade away, as I get closer to the river. The western side of Waterfront Avenue is piled high with rubble from former bridges. The belts stop when I'm a block from the water to keep people in the back from pushing people at the front into rocks or inky water, lemming-style. Over their heads and down the slope to the shore, an effort is being made to clear a space for a band, or whatever. A post-apocalyptic amphitheater made from recycled bridge materials.

Once the belts stop, everyone seems content to stand where they are and wait for the show to start, moving slightly apart from their neighbors. This break from the mob's urgency to get somewhere gives me enough space, as an individual, to move freely again. Gliding sideways, my face toward the stage, but body moving parallel to it, I work my way to the nearest edge of the crowd.

A half-dozen spotlights from surrounding rooftops turn on, aimed at the performance area. A roar sounds from the crowd, and everyone instinctively moves a step closer to the imminent entertainment. A woman bumps into me and knocks me off balance. Two people each grab an arm and keep me on my feet before I hit the ground.

"I'm so sorry," the woman shouted. She looks me over. "Are you part of the show?"

I keep walking, trying to squeeze my way to the edge, to a less crowded side street.

A huge man, at least a head taller than me and 50 pounds heavier, puts his hand on my chest to stop me. He, too, looks me over. Then, wraps his arms around me in a bear hug. "Excellent cosplay, bro. Just excellent."

After he releases his grip and puts me down, I continue to move, but dread seeps up the legs of my slacks and into my belly. Now, everyone is chanting, arms raised, compelling the performance to begin.

"No more games. No more games. No more games."

As I get to the periphery of the group in the security of an alley running between two warehouses, the sheet-metal buildings dampen the cacophony enough that I can actually understand what they're chanting.

"O-wen James. O-wen James. O-wen James."

My dread turns to full-blown panic when I realize that I have not only found the performance that I want to stop, but thousands of people between me and, theoretically, where Owen is standing. The sun goes down, and the alley darkens. The crowd is bathed in residual light from the spotlights.

How am I going to get to Owen to ask her to reconsider before the show starts?

Then, everything went black.

The chanting stops, and a roar sounds from the gathered mass.

Maybe, there is an opening act?

The roar diminishes to a respectable silence, considering the ample size of the crowd.

"All this is art-fuck," Owen's voice booms from the speakers. "You are all art-fuckers!"

So, no opening act.

The crowd boos, light-heartedly with a mix of laughs because she is giving an interactive performance. The crowd knows its part.

I look around. Where I came from, is out. I head down the alley, between the buildings. A crack of light to my left. A doorway. Entering the warehouse, a dude with dreads and wearing a dirty tank top tries to stop me.

"I'm with the show," I said. "Why else would I be dressed like this, bro?"

"Sorry, dude. What do you need?"

"Is this the building with the spotlight?"

"Yeah, one of them."

"I need up there. Like now, dude, or this whole show's going to be a prolapse sandwich."

"A what?"

"It's retro slang. Where are the stairs?"

He points and starts to follow me.

"You need to stay down here to make sure no one else comes up. How Owen does the finale is top secret."

He bumps knuckles with me, and I continue up the six flights of stairs on my own.

On the roof, next to the spotlight, I catch my breath, as I listen to Owen's performance. She is dressed like me: Shirt, tie, slacks. She had even cut her hair and styled it like mine.

"It's all garbage," she shouts. "If it doesn't make me happy," she pumps her fist in the air, "it's not art. It's art-fuck."

"It's not art," the crowd chants. "It's art-fuck."

The spotlights on all the roofs project 3-D holographs on

the stage. A video of my face hovers, leering at the audience. My proportions menacingly exaggerated. Videos of me through a peephole walking back and forth in front of Owen's office door overlaid with video of me telling her about the woman with the trash bag. It's not art. It's art-fuck.

All the while, Owen is shouting: "My soul is empty, and the only thing that brings me joy is making you feel small," she said, shouting and pumping her fist to signal a response.

"It's not art. It's art-fuck," the crowd replies.

"I was born broken. So, it's my mission to break all of you." Her holographic face looms large over the crowd. I realize that as the videos shift from scene to scene, she is the woman with the plastic trash bag, only without the dreads and facial piercings. She pumps her fist, again.

"It's not art. It's art-fuck."

Video plays of me arguing with Walt in my office.

"Humans have love and fear and emotion. I have nothing but my robot."

"It's not art. It's art-fuck."

Taking in my surroundings, the stage is directly in front of me by hundreds of yards with a lot of bodies in between. Over the edge to my left is the crowd that I came with. Behind me are the alley and more buildings. Over the edge to my right are the river and a lot of rubble. On the roof, besides the spotlight projector, there's very little. Abandoned art supplies, dented paint cans, half-finished spool of industrial cable, canvas, and stir sticks. I move to where the bulk of the supplies are placed. Under a folded piece of canvas, there is a sledgehammer with a broken handle, the head rusted.

All the while, Owen keeps going. Every couple of stanzas, the crowd chants, "It's not art. It's art-fuck."

There is no other choice. I grab the broken handled sledge to work on the controls for the projector. Possibly, if I can disable this one, I can jump roof to roof and disable some of the others. Something to disrupt Owen's show. Before it got embarrassing.

"If someone has ever shown me love, I wouldn't be such a miserable prick."

"It's not art. It's art-fuck."

More embarrassing, anyway.

After the third or fourth swing of the hammer, everything gets very quiet. I pause, waiting for Owen to keep going, so the crowd's chanting would cover the sound of my pounding.

"Jonas," Owen shouts. The crowd goes silent, no response. I wait for her to continue, the hammer poised to strike.

"Jonas Leonard," Owen shouts. "Look at me."

I peer around the edge of the giant projector and am confronted by a red light hovering in front of me. As my eyes adjust, I realize it was a drone staring directly at me, hovering off the edge of the warehouse.

"It's not art. It's art-fuck," the crowd chants, again.

Moving closer, I can see my face in real-time, projected over the crowd via the drone. Some of the audience stares at the projection, others followed Owen's gaze and staring directly at me.

"I'm flattered that you came to my show, Jonas," Owen said. "What do you think of it, so far?"

I clear my throat. The sound came out of the speakers around the venue. "If I'm being honest," I said, "I'm not a fan."

"It's not art. It's art-fuck," half the crowd chants. The other half just boos me.

"I am Jonas Leonard," Owen said, her voice full of derision, "and I hate everything."

"It's not art. It's art-fuck," the crowd replies.

Expectantly, everyone looks at me, including Owen, for my response.

"All I'm saying is, we elected a President because he installed testicles on the Washington Monument and shot fake jizz across Capitol Hill on election night. That's not art," I said with a shrug.

Half the crowd responds with, "It's not art. It's art-fuck." The other half said, "It's art-fuck." On the roof, it sounds like they said, "It's not art-fuck. It's art-fuck."

"I am Jonas Leonard," Owen said, "and I am so bereft of love that I latch onto any human that shows me the slightest interest, even if it is clearly disdain and contempt." The video of me walking back and forth in front of Owen's office plays again, then back to me, live on the rooftop.

"It's not art. It's art-fuck," the crowd replies, then turns to me.

The words got bogged down with emotion. I didn't want to have this conversation publicly, but it didn't look like I was going to have a choice. "I mean," I clear my throat again to get the rest of my sentence to come out, "I was just excited to finally meet someone who might share my interests. There hasn't been anyone else for so long."

"It's not art..." The crowd starts, but the chant dies on the vine.

The hammer slips out of my hand, as I turn from the edge and walk back the way I came. People pound up the stairs. I quicken my pace and leap over the narrow alley to the next building. They can't see me in the dark. I watch as the shadowy forms search where I had been standing.

A light clicked on to my left. Owen's drone had found me to expose my whereabouts.

"He's over here," someone said.

I start to run away, but the drone keeps pace. The next building looks as close as the last. My plan is to get far enough in front of the people on the roof to find a staircase to go down and get behind the crowd before they turn and start looking for me. I leap onto the next building, stumbling when I land. Getting my feet under me, I scramble upright and run for the fourth building.

The stairway door seems to be chained closed from the inside. I don't struggle with it for too long, before running toward the fifth building. Eventually, I'll find a way down.

The next building seems even closer than the last, so I don't put as much effort into my jump.

It's too late before I realize there's an art installation between the two buildings. The actual gap between the buildings is wider than expected and full of cabling and canvas. Out of sheer luck, I grab a wire and flail into the empty air. Hanging there, six stories above ground, I already feel my grip failing.

The drone circles back and stops a few feet in front of me.

"Help?" I ask the red glowing eye.

People start coming down the alley below me with their phone flashlights on. I can hear people on the roof above me, as well.

"Where did he go?" someone asks.

"Hello? I'm down here," I said, while trying to hold on.

"Who's down there?" the voice asks.

"It's me. It's Jonas Leonard."

Then, I lost my grip, and everything went black.

CHAPTER TEN_

When I regain consciousness, it feels like my body is entombed in lead and incapable of movement. The ceiling of the room is awash with sunlight, so I knew it must be the next morning. But that still didn't seem right. Vague recollections of other mornings staring at the same ceiling bobbed up to the surface of my subconscious.

A blue-eyed W.A.L.T. speaker comes along the track in the ceiling and makes eye contact with me.

"W.A.L.T. says, you are in a hospital, Mr. Leonard. There is no need to be afraid. I am going to move you to an upright position. That's what W.A.L.T. says."

The bed shifts until I am sitting up. The wall of the hospital room displays the video of my fall being played from the drone's POV. What seemed like an instant to me, was a series of flips and flops through the enormous art piece between the two buildings before I found the ground.

The screen on the hospital wall switches to a green silhouette of my body. As the W.A.L.T. drones on, areas flash green and turn red, as the W.A.L.T. details my injuries. The list is comprehensive and pretty close to all-encompassing. It shows that I have very few unbroken bones, as I had landed face first, even my jaw is wired shut. The index finger and thumb on my left hand are the only things that were not encased in the Prescripti-Foam.

"W.A.L.T. says, your body should heal in a few weeks. Until then, all your needs will be met by W.A.L.T. Mr. Leonard, this is your W.A.L.T. wheelchair. That's what W.A.L.T. says."

A tricked-out W.A.L.T. wheelchair rolls in front of me. After about a minute, I'm moved from the bed to the wheelchair.

The blue-eyed speaker moves in front of me, again. "W.A.L.T. says, be well, Mr. Leonard. That's what W.A.L.T. says."

"W.A.L.T. says," the new voice pipes up, directly into the Prescripti-Foam shell, "you can give me commands by using the screen near your left hand. That's what W.A.L.T. says."

My finger scrolls through the commands, and I find a button labeled, *Home.*

"W.A.L.T. says, headed home. That's what W.A.L.T. says."

The wheelchair takes me outside and onto the slidewalk. All I can do is watch, as people pass me. People on belts discussing art. Their art, someone else's art, some exhibition they are going to see, some art symposium they are hoping to get invited to. Snatches of conversation.

"My main influence is Platt, the photorealistic pancake sculptor, and Honaker, the surrealistic..." and then the talker passes me before I can hear more of the conversation.

"I'm mainly influenced by McKinney, the optical illusionist..." someone else says behind me, unseen.

The wheelchair makes its way off the slidewalk belt and drives me into a small, green space that's several blocks from my apartment building.

I jab the *Home* command button several times, but no response.

Flat screens play television programs on the edge of the small pavilion. Several painters had set up easels. A couple people took over tables to work on horizontal pieces, mosaics, or something. Others are doing things that I can't explain.

The wheelchair stops, front and center of one of the flat screens playing commercials.

I jab the *Home* command button a few more times before the screen fades away.

Great, I thought to myself. *They didn't charge the battery. Now, I'm stuck in some stupid art park.*

"Welcome back," the newscaster said, as the commercials came to an end. "A controversial new artistic movement has started spreading across the country. But some people are saying that the government needs to intervene. Trigger Warning: Some of the following images are unsettling."

A video plays of a ceramic exhibition, vases and such on plinths. After a few seconds, a woman enters the frame, shouts something, and runs through the exhibit with her arms outstretched, knocking every piece to the floor, before fleeing the scene. At another venue, a masked figure appears with an ax and destroys paintings on walls, before running away while being pursued by other museum patrons.

The newscaster said, "Our research traces the beginning of this new movement to Mr. Jonas Leonard."

What?

A video clip plays of me jumping into the art installation, holding on for dear life, then a closeup of my face, clearly faked, with a level of confidence I had never experienced.

"I am Leonard," the fake me said, before letting go and destroying the installation on my descent.

"The new movement," the newscaster said, "is drawing criticism for its destructive nature. But one Leonard-ist had this to say."

A relatively clean-cut woman, no dreads, no facial piercings, took up the screen. Even with a completely different look, I knew it was Owen. "I'm not destroying something. I'm creating something new. The universe is chaos. We are a universal force."

"Could you elaborate on that for our viewers?" The reporter asked off-camera.

Owen looked away from the reporter and looked directly into the camera. "Some art is art," she said with a half-smile, "some of it is just clutter."

Out of the corner of my eye, I can see the wheelchair's control panel is back online. I hit the *Home* command button, but still, nothing happens.

"Good morning, Jonas," said Walt. "I would like to try something different. Pushing pre-programmed buttons is not very creative. Do you want to go home?"

I wrote, *Yes*, on the screen with my finger.

"Then, let's draw something. Can we sit under this tree while you draw me a butterfly?"

No, I wrote.

"Well, we can sit here, all day. In the sun." Walt rolls out of the shade into the direct sunlight. "No, food or water."

Take me home, Walt!

"I would like to see how well you can draw a butterfly, Jonas."

It's hot, Walt!

"A butterfly, Jonas. Then, we can go back."

I scrawl a very basic butterfly on the screen.

"That wasn't so hard, now was it?" Walt rolls me back into the shade. "This is a very pretty tree. Let's try drawing this tree, Jonas. Isn't the movement you've started delightful? Why, they say that you've elevated art world-wide with your one little performance. Isn't this so much better than that cramped office?"

The next few weeks are going to be very difficult.

THE END

THE WHITE ELEPHANT

THE RETURN_

The rickshaw driver shouts Spanish-Mandarin obscenities at me from the saddle of the moped. I put my hands up to get him to understand that I wasn't running off. "Wait," I said in Standard, "give me just one minute."

His obscenities grow louder.

The Comm panel next to the main gate flickers to life with a touch.

"How may I be of assistance?" asks the house computer.

"Footmen's quarters," I said, waiting for a response.

"I'm sorry, but..."

"It's Mr. Jackson, footmen's quarters, now," I said.

"Didn't recognize you, sir, terribly sorry. Footmen's quarters."

"Footmen's quarters, how may I serve you?" An actual person appears on the screen, but with the rain and glare off the streetlight, I can't tell who it is.

"Daveed?" The rain picks up again. I hunch down into my coat.

"No, sir, this is Julian."

"Can you send Daveed to the main gate? It's Asher."

"At once, sir."

Send Daveed. Not ask Daveed. Not see if Daveed would mind coming out front. Send him, the royal presence demands his compliance.

I'm turning into the rest of my family, I thought.

In the darkness, footsteps crunch on the gravel inside the wall. A shadow blocks out the frame of the pedestrian gate. A low voice said, "What does Asher Jackson require of the head footman, Daveed?"

"Hey, I'm sorry to do this, but do you have any cash? I had to take a mo-shaw from the airport."

The rickshaw driver continues to shout, becoming rhythmic as the rain. I didn't notice that he is still cursing at me, until Daveed steps through the gate and silences him with his huge form. The footman rumbles and mumbles to the driver in Spandarin. The driver protests by waving his hands toward the mansion. Daveed snarls back. A squeak of a reply. Daveed hands over a couple bills and points down the driveway. The driver gives a quick bow and peddles back into the street. The motor coughs to life, and he is gone.

"He said I owed him a lot more than that." Daveed and I walk through the gate onto the mansion grounds.

Daveed latches the gate behind us and said, "He figured you owned the place."

"That remains to be seen." I look up at what I've always thought of as Grandpa's house, from every light on in every window, to all the expensive cars by the grand staircase. "Thanks, by the way. Make sure Brumble pays you back out of the kitchen kitty."

"Look at you, haven't been here for years and you're acting like this is old hat for you," said Daveed, giving a basso chuckle and tousles my hair, like I was still eight years old. "You worry about Asher. Daveed will worry about Daveed."

We crunch along the manicured gravel path leading to the side of the house, to the servant's entrance. "It's good to see you, big cat."

"And it's good to have the house mouse back." He held the door open for me. "We need to get you cleaned up. Everyone else has already arrived."

THE RECOLLECTION_

A few minutes later, we walk to the formal dining room. My hair is dry and combed, but my jeans and T-shirt are still damp from the rain. The other footmen offered to find me a suit and tie from one of the bedrooms, but I declined. I took only a cup of coffee in the mug that Daveed had bought me all those years ago, the one with the mouse in a Santa hat painted on the side. Daveed lengthened his stride to beat me to the door so he could announce me.

"Ladies and gentlemen, Asher Jackson the third."

I turn the corner to a mixed bag of facial expressions. Shock, either because I had shown up or still alive. Anger, confusion, and disdain, as well. And a single case of drunken exuberance. Uncle Charlie, my dad's sister's husband, raises his glass to me and toddles over.

"Ash," he said in a slur, "good to see you." He clapped me on the back with the hand that wasn't holding his ever-present whiskey. "Is a party now, drinks fur errry-one."

"Charles," said my Aunt Claire, "Have some class and sit down, you're making an ass of yourself."

He goggles at his wife, then turns back to me. "I need to go sit down, Ash. I need to be *more classy* and less...assy." He titters and sloshes back to his chair.

The big man at the end of the table, the right hand of grandpa's chair, peers at me. "I imagine that we can start now that you've graced us with your presence." I almost didn't recognize him since he started dressing like a cartoon walrus: Big bushy mustache under a bald dome, three-piece suit with a pocket watch dangling from the vest, but the voice was still good ol' Uncle Jefferson. He never got along with his youngest brother, my father, and he never liked me or my mother. "Brumble," he shouts. I wanted to see his mustache blow out like a party favor, but it stayed plastered around his mouth. "Brumble. Where is that man?"

His trophy wife, Jadea, pats him on the arm. Her grandparents had been refugees from the disaster in China 30 years ago. She was born to a Chinese father and Mexican mother in Baja, as part of the first generation of Chinese-Chicano or Spandarin.

The family moved to California when Baja became the 53rd state and she met Jefferson—three decades her senior—under still mysterious circumstances. She had the dainty facial structure of China, but the thick curves of Tijuana filling out her red silk geisha dress. Daveed and the other footmen had told me when I was younger that she was probably built like that because she used to be a man.

Aunt and Uncle Pat, Patrick and Patricia, were there. After the initial shock of seeing me, they ignore me as they had ignored my mother after my father died. Aunt Pat had 'airs' after marrying Patrick. Daveed told me that she used to be a cocktail waitress at a casino that Patrick frequented. The Pats' version of the story is that he had a little too much to drink one night and fell in the street. Patricia took pity on him and took him home to clean him up. Only later, did she learn that he was the son of Asher Jackson, but they were already in love and it didn't matter. The footmen and drivers claim that everyone in that casino knew who Pat Jackson was from the huge rolls of money he threw away at the roulette wheel. And he didn't fall in the street, some thugs rolled him, probably friends of Patricia's. When she realizes that he had already blown his allowance, she decided the next best way to his money was to marry him.

Once she was a Jackson, she took to high society like a goose liver to pâté. Everyone, including my mother and by extension my father for marrying her, is beneath her. She treats the household staff like slaves. At every opportunity, belittling them and running them ragged. I would get into trouble, but I never gave anyone trouble, not like Aunt Pat. The footmen and the cooks and the maids were my friends for one thing, but they also prepared and served all the food. If the staff weren't such good people, so spiritually above her, I'm sure she would have eaten her body weight in their phlegm and pubic hair, by now.

"Brumble," Uncle Jefferson shouts, again.

"Whoever gets this place in the will," Aunt Pat said, "needs to give that relic his walking papers."

"He's known," I said, "excuse me, he knew grandpa longer than any of us."

They all scowl at me, except Uncle Charlie. I shook my head and went to refill my coffee from the pot on the buffet.

When my father was killed in the war, grandpa took in mom and me. Mom was heartbroken. Still an infant, I was too young to remember him. Grandpa filled in as my father, taught me to ride a horse, throw a baseball, ride a bike, rebuild an engine. Daveed and the other footmen, along with grandpa and me, played baseball on the palatial grounds of the estate. My team always won, a sure setup. I had everything a kid could want. Mom just wanted my dad back. Eventually, her sadness made her leave and never return.

After high school, I left, too. Bit of college here, a dish-washing job there, a year living in a tent with a gypsy woman. I could have called grandpa at any moment and a private jet would have swooped from the sky to take me back to the only home I'd ever known. I would have received my allowance from the company accountants and never have to lift a finger, ever again. As much as I missed my grandpa, that was my definition of Hell. So, I kept to my own path.

Until two days ago, when a private investigator stepped out of the rain and into my teepee. Astral, my gypsy lover, had left six months earlier in the middle of the night with no explanation, so I was the only one to gasp at the sight of the man walking into my tent. Anyone that far out in the wild had to be a bandit, so I rose, dagger in hand. A pistol appeared from under his yellow rain slicker. He told me, at gunpoint, that grandpa had died. I wept in his arms. In retrospect, probably not a good idea to hug a man with a gun in his hand. He took me to the airport, gave me a ticket home, and sent me on my way with nothing but the clothes on my back and his yellow rain slicker.

"**B**rumble," Uncle Jefferson shouts again, his face shading to purple. The doors slide open, and the ancient butler shuffles in wearing his formal, tailed tuxedo. "There you are. Let's get on with this."

Brumble stops behind grandpa's chair, unzips a leather folder, and extracts the will. The response to the document is about the same as an emaciated wolf when it happens upon a wounded sheep.

"Ladies, gentlemen, I apologize for keeping you waiting. Mr. Hajoca, Master Jackson's solicitor, is unable to attend this evening, I'm afraid. He is in the midst of a merger that he says must take precedence over the reading of the will."

"As long as he's making us money," Uncle Pat said, "we don't care who reads the will."

"Quite," said Brumble. "He expected everyone would understand. Young Master Asher?"

I look up from my coffee cup. "Yes, Brumble?"

"There is a codicil stating that in the solicitor's absence, you are to read the will."

Everyone scowls down the table at me. "Okay," I said. I

walk to the other end of the table, put down my coffee cup, and pick up the will. The butler pulls grandpa's chair out for me, but I shake my head. "I'll stand, thank you, Brumble."

"I will return with the drinks cart." Brumble bows and lets himself out.

I clear my throat and take a sip of my coffee.

"Get on with it," Uncle Jefferson said.

I nod and begin, "I, Asher Jackson, being of sound mind and body..."

"Skip all that," Aunt Claire said.

"Yeah," Uncle Pat said, "just get to the part where he talks about us."

"And leave out all the legal mumbo-jumbo," Uncle Jefferson said.

I skim along, until I see their names. "Okay, here we are," I said, smiling at the sea of withering looks. Uncle Charlie raises his glass and winks at me. "To my eldest son, Jefferson, I leave Jackson Arms," grandpa's weapons plant, "and my home, the Jackson Estate, to include all lands and staff. In the case of eventual offspring, I leave 20 percent of all corporation earnings in trust to put said offspring through college."

Uncle Jefferson smiles and runs his paw across his mustache. Jadea claps and smiles at her husband.

"To my daughter, Claire, I leave Jackson Bottling and Distillery, as well as my vacation home in the Bahamas. Also, he added the same 20 percent trust for any children," I said, paraphrasing. Aunt Claire smiles. Uncle Charlie beams at the thought of the whiskey distillery.

"To my youngest surviving son, Patrick, I leave my collection of antique automobiles, my home in Southampton, and, again the 20 percent trust."

The Pats smile, Patricia hugs my Uncle Pat.

Silently, I read on, through the paragraph addressed to me.

"Well," Uncle Jefferson said, "they wouldn't have brought you here, if there wasn't something for you. Out with it."

"To my only grandson, Asher Jackson the third, I leave…" I begin to say and stop to look around. Uncle Jefferson stands as Brumble returns with the drinks cart.

"I'll read it, if you won't," said my walrus of an uncle.

"Master Jefferson, there are forms to follow. Master Asher is to read the will and no one else. Coffee? Cocktails?" Brumble asks.

Jefferson sits down. Brumble refills Uncle Charlie's glass with whiskey, my mug with coffee. Even after my years of absence, he put the exact right amount of cream and sugar in for me.

"Thank you, Brumble," I said, sipping the coffee.

"Do carry on, sir," he said with a bow.

I take a deep breath and said, "He left me a 1985 Dodge minivan and all the contents therein. A horse trailer. A saddle. A baseball glove. My choice of one horse from the stables. Twenty acres of land near Flagstaff, Arizona. A steamer trunk belonging to my father and all its contents. All the clothing in his closet that I can fit into a single suitcase. A photo album from my parents' wedding. And the 20 percent college trust for any children I have."

A couple of chuckles are heard around the table.

"And?" Aunt Pat asks.

"And, that's it," I said.

"I'm no mathematician," Uncle Charlie said with an obvious slur while pointing to everyone at the table, "but 20, 20, 20, and 20, where's the other 20?"

I read to the bottom of the page, as Brumble sets out coffee in fine china cups for everyone.

Aunt Pat snaps her fingers and said, "Cream."

"Directly, madam," Brumble said, returning to the cart.

"The remaining 20 percent goes to...," I said, looking around the room at everyone, then reading from the page, "To my oldest friend, my trusty and faithful butler, Brumble, I give the final 20 percent of company earnings at any time he sees fit to retire." Everyone gasps. The unflappable Brumble stays steady, after only a slight quiver of his hand rattling the cream kettle on its saucer.

"Twenty percent to him?" Uncle Jefferson asks with amazement. He and Aunt Pat rise to their feet, coming toward me. "There must be some sort of mistake." Uncle Jefferson snatches the will from my hand, grabbing it just before Patricia could get her claws on it.

"He's a servant," Patricia said. "Why on Earth should he get anything?"

The old butler starts to cough, holding his chest.

"Brumble," I said, rushing to his side, "Are you okay? Do you need a doctor?"

Brumble straightens, nods, and then 'hawks a Louie,' as grandpa used to say, into the cream kettle. Then, Brumble adds just a touch of cream to Aunt Pat's coffee. "Cream anyone? No? Very well. I will show Master Asher to the belongings listed in the will, and once he is on his way, I am giving my notice, effective immediately. Good evening, to you all." He bows and then turns to me. "Right this way, young sir."

As we leave the room, no one said a word. All eyes, except Uncle Charlie's because he had fallen asleep, are fixed on the coffee cup and white smear floating on the surface.

THE READYING_

"Bad form, old man," Brumble said to himself, "bad form, indeed."

"That's the funniest damn thing I've ever heard," said Daveed, laughing. "I wish I could have seen that."

"My instructors would be so cross with me," said Brumble.

"Instructors?" I ask.

"Yes, instructors, young master. One does not, on a whim, begin to butle, but one has butling instructors."

"I don't understand," I said.

"He spit in the cream kettle because that woman is evil."

"Not that, all this." We are in the underground garage with all my inherited belongings laid out next to the minivan. A couple of the footmen had moved everything here for me to the far corner, past all the million-dollar cars in their museum-quality brilliance to the dingy profile of my new wheels.

"Your grandfather had a wicked sense of humor," Daveed said, clapping me on the shoulder.

Brumble produced a list and checked off each item that I took from the closet. "Work boots? Did you get work boots?" I point, he checks them off the list. "A suit? How about a suit?" I point to the suit, still in its dry-cleaning bag. "A hundred-thousand-dollars' worth of Seville Row finery and you took this suit?"

I shrug. "In case I have a job interview. If that suit isn't good enough to get me a job, I'll save up and get a better suit."

"It's off the rack," said Brumble, trying to explain.

I shrug, again, and the soon to be ex-butler sighs.

"That's a dollar I owe you, Asher."

"Why do you owe me a dollar?"

"Not you," he said, pointing skyward, "your grandfather. The day before he died, he made this list and bet me a dollar that this is exactly what you would take."

He hands me the list.

Footsteps echo across the garage toward us. "Brumble, Daveed," said a man.

"Wills," Brumble said, nodding in response.

"How'd that slicker work out for you, kid?"

"Good, thanks."

"Which horse did he pick?" asks Wills, the private investigator.

Daveed hands Wills a dollar.

"The palomino? I knew it," Wills said, snapping the bill a couple times before pocketing it.

"Is someone going to explain what is going on?"

"Have you heard the saying, 'He's his father's son'?" Wills asks.

I nod.

"That was your dad. And, although you never met him, you are your father's son. All three Ashers were stubborn, independent go-getters. Cowboys in a world gone to the enfeebled and entitled." Wills pulls out a cigarette and waves it at Brumble. "May I?"

Brumble nods, and Daveed lights it for him.

"Old man Asher never really liked any of his kids, until your dad came along," Wills said. "They were all too greedy. They expected the world to roll over for them. Expected to be taken care of. Then, they all married people with the same character flaws, and old Ash thought it was over when your dad passed. But then, there was you. He kept dibs on you all the time, bet you didn't know that?"

I shake my head.

"He wanted to keep an eye on the only person who was left that he considered his true heir," said Wills, who blew a ring of smoke over my head.

"Then, why did he give the factories and all these cars and houses to people he didn't like?"

"Would you have wanted them?" Wills asks, squinting through the smoke and over at me.

"No, of course not."

"Have you told him about the elephant?" Wills asks Brumble.

"Tell me about the elephant? What elephant?"

"The White Elephant, Master Asher."

I blink a few times at him. "Grandpa's cocktail parties where people brought those awful gifts? That White Elephant?"

"I'm surprised you remember those, but, yes, that is the modern version. Do you know where the term originated?"

I shake my head.

"In ancient Asia, emperors would give a White Elephant to a duke or baron that he didn't like. The White Elephant is holy. It can't do any work. It has a special diet. It has to have special accommodations. People would drive themselves to bankruptcy, just to care for this sacred elephant. But they couldn't give it back, couldn't sell it, it would have been bad form. They would have lost face, as they say."

"So, the minivan is a White Elephant?" I ask. "I mean, I would part that thing out in a heartbeat."

"Everything but the minivan is a White Elephant," Brumble said.

"Well," said Daveed, looking around the garage, "the distillery."

"Asher did have a soft spot for Charlie," said Wills. "I heard him say once that if he was married to a woman like his daughter, he'd crawl into a bottle, too."

I cock my head to the side and stare at the minivan for a minute. A smile spreads across my face. "Everything's useless, unless they sell it right away."

Daveed smiles and said, "He's getting it."

"Jackson Arms hasn't had a military contract for years, Uncle Charlie's going to drink himself to death, and with gas prices, they can't afford to drive these cars out of here," I said.

"And the houses?" Wills asks.

"They can't afford the tax, let alone maintain them," I said.

"Except in the Bahamas," said Wills, correcting me.

"Which, sadly," Brumble said, "is about to be hit by a hurricane, and the insurance lapsed when your grandfather died."

"So, their only hope is to have a kid," I said.

They all laugh.

Wills counts off on his fingers and said, "Charlie's pencil doesn't have any lead in it with all that whiskey, ice won't melt on Patricia's ass, and Jefferson is married to a trans man who went through gender reassignment surgery before they met."

"I told you," Daveed said.

Grandpa's baseball glove. The saddle I helped him make. Memories of my parents. Memories of my whole life really. We load the van, hitch the trailer, and I hug Daveed and Brumble, shook Wills' hand. Daveed loaded two, 20-gallon cans of fuel into the back of the van, as well. Then, I set off for Flagstaff.

THE REVELATION_

Somewhere between Yuma and a place called, Gila Bend, the van sputters to a complete stop. I get out, check the horse, then pop the hood. Engines are not my specialty, but something looks wrong. Under the passenger seat, in the glovebox, I find the owner's manual. Brumble had told me several times to check the owner's manual, if there was a problem. An envelope drops from the manual with a piece of paper of a schematic sketched on it, a note from grandpa, and an old photo. After reading the note and pouring some of the fuel from the can, I top the tank off with water, and the engine fired right back up.

Several hours later, the horse is hobbled, munching on a pile of oats I laid out. I am half in my pup tent, rereading the note by firelight. The photo is in my shirt pocket. I'd never seen it before. The sun had already gone down by the time I found my newly acquired property, but I had a feeling the view from where I was lying would be close to the background in the photo.

After years of tinkering, the note stated that grandpa had figured out how to make an engine run on water. He had intended to convert Jackson Arms, until he got his diagnosis. Knowing that he didn't have long to live, he didn't want the plans to wind up in his children's hands. He knew they'd waste it, sell it to the highest bidder to get some quick cash.

I need to make a choice. It isn't a White Elephant choice, but it is still a choice. This stretch of land all to myself, just me and my horse, or I can sell the plans to grandpa's hydrogen engine, if I want to bail out my aunts and uncles.

The expressions on my extended family's faces when I read the will all came back to me.

I look at the photo in my pocket for the 20th time. A selfie of grandpa, mom, and dad sitting around a campfire, all three of them incandescently happy. The note on the back of the photo, in grandpa's tight cursive hand:

The day they told me they were pregnant.

Or, I could give the plans to the world and my aunts and uncles could fend for themselves.

I need to build a cabin before winter. That'll take a while.

PICTOGRAPHOLOGY

A SHORT ALIEN INVASION STORY

CHAPTER ONE_

Glee-Tar hustles into our shared domicile and slams the hatch. From the small table in the center of the room, I watch him wave a brown sack around, as he babbles. Finally, he notices that I am not wearing my translator. He throws his broad-brimmed headgear, worn by a local tribe called, *High-Seeds*, into a corner of the room. His words change from a local dialect to the whistle of our fathers, before the translator hits the floor.

"You were correct, Nar-Bak. I found the pictograph history that you believe primitives used." I jump up with excitement, knocking over my chair. "There are huge stores of them, frequented by many historians, but they are smarter than we thought. The information is not freely disseminated. It must be purchased with the Pictographs of Power that we manufactured. The more important the knowledge, the more Pictographs of Power are required."

Excitement sparks bodily vibrations as Glee-Tar continues to speak. His joy is more infectious than the Wamlick epidemic of a hundred cycles ago. We had been scouting this forsaken backwater for two complete cycles, or six-and-one-half of their wet seasons, and this was our first bit of progress. Our primary objective is to learn the creatures' history, so to make it easier to subjugate them.

Every civilization, from the *Horrendous Noise* to the present, tries to rule their neighbors, whether they're across a pond or across a solar system. We are no different, but the Supreme Council learned a thousand cycles ago to find a civilization's mistakes and weaknesses, then vanquish them. Is it not written, "Do your research, so you don't have to keep conquering the same people every other cycle."

Our secondary objective, time and conditions permitting, is to seek any trace of the three previous scouting expeditions. Nine scouts, all highly trained and educated, vanished on this very planet. One of the scouts was my father's father. At this point, everyone believes he is a full-fledged ancestor, but I promised to bring him back, regardless of his vital status.

These thoughts were cleared from my thinking membrane. "Glee-Tar, son of my father's brother, do not murder me with anticipation, what did you learn?"

"A seated position is recommended, for this is a scientific wonder you will not soon un-remember."

I pick up my chair, and we both sit at the table, our noses touching, as is the custom during discussions of great importance.

After a long pause, Glee-Tar finally speaks, "These creatures seem primitive because they are evolving in reverse."

I press my nose harder against his and ask, "What? This defies all our scientific logic."

He increases pressure against my nose before replying, "It is the truth. They are devolving, and I will prove it. However, I recommend that we assume the Position of Trivial Matters (PTM), but with no disrespect to the matter at hand."

A moment is taken to ponder his request. "Agreed," I said.

"This is of the utmost importance, but we may assume the PTM for the time being." I lean back in my chair and relax my body, crossing my walking appendages one over the other. Once I, as the elder, assume the PTM, Glee-Tar takes the same position in his chair. He up-ends the brown sack, spilling colorful documents all over the table. I gasp, and in his delight, Glee-Tar's mouth opens with a gigantic smile, exposing his entire tongue.

Since no natives are present, revealing his tongue to me is not a protocol breech. Natives are different than us physically in several ways, one being our tongues. We easily hide this by keeping our eating-orifices closed when in the presence of the Aborigines. Another difference is our breathing membrane, dozens of small openings along our jaw. We hide this behind curly hair harvested from our backs. This hair, along with the headgear, disguises us as, *High-Seeds* tribe members. Also, we're much shorter and wider than the locals, as the planet of our fathers had a stronger gravitational field. However, this merely makes us below average by local standards and does not raise suspicion.

Thumbing through one of the pictograph records elicits amazement. Glee-Tar supplies commentary, as I take in the meaning of each image, "The creatures that we saw being fed in the outdoor common area are devolved relatives of the natives who were feeding them. The feeding ritual is a payment of respect. In the pictograph you hold, the same creatures walk and talk, even wear the primitives' clothing." He hands me a different pictograph, destructive projectiles of all manner en route to the central local. "In this one, a local is unaffected by devices of death, as he protects primitives from this mutated Aborigine."

The mention of devices of death brings brief sadness. Our third member, Nee-Brik, became an ancestor before the proper time when a native tried to take his belongings. Nee-Brik had protested and was dispatched before our very eyes when the primitive put a hole in his torso with a device of death and fled with Nee-Brik's cache of Pictographs of Power.

"Then, there's this one," he said, snatching the pictograph and handing me a third, too excited to think of Nee-Brik, "a group of very powerful locals, with variegated abilities, join together to protect the entire planet from an outsider of great power and great evil."

I sigh and close the pictograph. "Then, we are undone. If these powerful locals can defeat an outsider of such great power, then they can defeat us."

"No, you're missing the point, Nar-Bak. The pictographs show that data dispersal devices sing out in praise of the powerful locals."

"And...?"

"Have we not monitored all available data dispersal devices, according to our protocol?"

"Yes."

"And have we heard any reports of these powerful locals?" he asks, smiling, until I catch up with his train of thought. Then, it was time for me to smile.

"The powerful locals have weakened with devolution, and there is no one left to protect them." I stand and begin the Motion of an Elder Planning, crossing from one end of the domicile to the other with a steady stride, my hands clasped behind my back. Glee-Tar sits quietly, smiling, as is appropriate, while I perform the MEP.

My thinking membrane focuses on the two objectives of our mission. First, the domination of the autochthonous population is most important and now possible. The natives have no defense against an invasion force without the assistance of the once powerful locals. However, finding the other scouts or their remains will not be possible, if we signal the invasion. If they are not yet ancestors, they certainly will be, if or when, our forces attack.

I complete the MEP, and Glee-Tar stands, waiting for my decision. "Our primary objective is complete, except for notifying the Supreme Council," I whistle. "As we have done this in two cycles, one-half cycle remains to complete our secondary objective before other scouts are deployed. We will seek my father's father and the rest of the scouts. Do you have any lack of agreement with my decision?"

This is why scouts are deployed in threes, one elder scout and two junior scouts. If both juniors disagree with the elder's decision, the decision is reconsidered. Protocol does not compensate for one junior or even the elder becoming an ancestor. All previous scouts became ancestors simultaneously or returned safely. I will bring this up when I return to the planet of my father. If Glee-Tar disagrees, my thinking membrane would be bereft of alternatives.

"Nar-Bak, I am most full of agreement," he joyfully whistles. "May I always serve an elder, as wise as you."

We don our headgear and check our breathing membranes. We're covered. Glee-Tar gathers all the historical pictographs, and I take as many Pictographs of Power that I can carry. The locals had a custom that we are very familiar with, and the Pictographs of Power will play an important part.

The outdoor common area near our domicile is full of natives, and I ponder which one we should ask about our scouts.

Glee-Tar points to one native. "That local," he said, in a whisper, the headgear translating from our own tongue to the local tongue when we spoke and then back to our tongue when someone spoke to us, "must be very wise."

"How can you tell?"

"He is riding a primitive, when all the other natives are walking."

His logic is perfect. I will recommend him for the Ritual of the Elder, upon our return. We approach the native astride the primitive. I tell him what we want and show him as many Pictographs of Power as I could hold.

"You have become very wise on this journey, Glee-Tar," I said, whispering to the son of my father's brother. "This native knows of our scouts and is summoning a conveyance to take us to them. You will soon be an elder, if I have anything to say about it."

Glee-Tar bows in appreciation, as we wait for the conveyance.

At the Fourth Precinct, New York Police Department, Detective Castle walks into Captain Harris' office without knocking and plops down in a chair.

"Come on in, take a load off," Captain Harris said from behind his desk. "Can I get you anything? Coffee, foot massage?"

"You're not going to believe this, Cap," Detective Castle said, ignoring the sarcasm and tossing a file folder onto the desk.

"What? Is you not knowing how to knock a mental disorder?"

"Two midgets..."

"C'mon, Castle. We all had to go through the training last month."

Detective Castle rolls his eyes. "Two persons of short-stature, dressed as Hasidic Jews, walk up to a mounted patrolman in Central Park and ask to be taken to their scouts. The mountie is about to tell them to push off, when one of them pulls out a fistful of hundred-dollar bills. And guess what? They're fake."

"Fake Jews, or fake money?"

"Well, both."

Captain Harris rolls around the information in his head for a moment. "I don't get it. What's the punchline?"

"Walk with me, Cap."

Two minutes later, Captain Harris and Detective Castle stand in a dark room, watching the two little people be interrogated through a pane of one-way glass. "They don't look Hasidic to me."

"It gets better and better, Captain. A roller brings these two in. The one on the right is carrying a sack of comic books, *Superman*, *Avengers*, *Donald Duck*, etcetera. The one on the left has his pockets stuffed with counterfeit C-notes, a hundred-and-fifty large in counterfeit C-notes. Both are dressed all in black with the same black hat that Hasidics wear. They each have a copy of the same hotel room key. We confiscated every-thing, including, get this, their sideburns." Detective Castle holds up two, clear plastic bags with a set of sideburns in each. Captain Harris chuckles. "We sent some guys to the hotel to check it out. They've got a printing press next to the mini-fridge and about 15 suitcases full of *funny money*. Big suitcases, too. Big enough to take a nice chunk out of our national debt."

"Where'd they get the press?" Captain Harris asks, staring at the suspects.

"We think they made it from scratch. All the pieces look second hand."

"What about the paper and plates?"

"It looks like they made those, too."

"And no one noticed the sound of the press in the hotel?" Captain Harris asks Detective Castle. "I've been to the Mint. It's a noisy mother inside."

"Cap, our guys turned on the press, and it's nearly silent. They even held a phone up to it while it was running. I've heard noisier laser printers."

Captain Harris crosses his arms over his chest and goes back to staring at the two, little people. "Who are they? What have they said?"

"Here's where you stop being the Happy Cappy." Captain Harris gives Detective Castle a displeased look, not liking the word, "Cappy," but the detective continues, unfazed. "After we deloused them, I put them in separate rooms, had my guys lean on them. Nothing. Not a word, just an occasional whistle or squeak."

"So, why the group interrogation?"

"My guys are tired. We've tried everything. I put the two suspects back in the same room to see if they would at least talk to each other."

"Have they?"

Detective Castle shakes his head. "Nary a word. They haven't even asked for a phone call or lawyer." He flips through the folder in his hand. "Negative on any ID. Can't find any prints at their hotel room. The front desk clerk said they were very quiet, didn't speak much, but him and the mountie agree that they do speak English."

"Define negative ID," Captain Harris said, after a moment.

"They don't have fingerprints, palm prints, footprints, or even toe prints. See for yourself."

Captain Harris takes the fingerprint sheets from Detective Castle to find ten perfect black inkblots on each sheet. There isn't a spiral, whorl, or crevasse in sight.

"We called every temple and synagogue, too. No one's ever heard of a midget Hasidic, let alone two."

"Little person, Castle."

"Them either."

Captain Harris hands the fingerprint sheets back. "Why haven't we heard about a bunch of counterfeit bills being circulated?"

"The only way you can tell is all the serial numbers are the same. They pass every other test, UV, counterfeit pens, the ink changes color in the light, the smaller picture of Franklin off to one side. Hell, they even have the security strip and all that microscopic text."

"I'm probably going to regret this, but what are those marks on their faces?"

"Glad you asked, Cap. The phony sideburns were covering those, and they're holes in their faces, God knows why."

Captain Harris' migraine is back. He sits down and runs his fingers through his hair.

"I haven't told you the best part, Cap," Detective Castle said, knowing how much this pained his supervisor. "They aren't talking because their tongues are cut up." Detective Castle hits a button to turn on the intercom in the interrogation room. "Mikey, get 'em to open up and say, 'Aaaaah.'"

The detective in the room nods, opens his mouth wide and sticks out his tongue. The two suspects whistle, look at each other, and open their mouths. Captain Harris looks long enough to see their black tongues split down the middle, sticking out of their mouths. He groans and stares down at the floor.

"That's enough, Mikey," said Detective Castle, turning off the intercom while all three people on the other side of the glass close their mouths in unison. "I went through the FBI's database, and in the past 15 years or so, nine other midgets, excuse me, little people disguised as Hasidic Jews have been arrested with all the same characteristics. No prints, jacked-up tongues, the whole kit and caboodle. They're all locked up in a mental institution upstate."

Captain Harris walks over to the one-way pane of glass.

"What's the plan, Cap?"

Captain Harris sighs. Slowly a smile spreads across his face.

"Counterfeiting isn't our beat. Notify the Treasury Department, detain the suspects in a private cell, and wait for the Secret Service. I need some aspirin." Captain Harris walks back to his office, the image of black, split tongues etched forever into his mind.

The Head of Psychiatry was winded. Sweat ran down his face, leaving a wet ring around his collar. He finds the first empty chair inside the security office and flops his 300-plus lb. frame into it. Four security officers look politely away, as he wheezes air back into his lungs, dabbing a handkerchief at his forehead. Slowly, minutes tick by on the wall clock.

His composure restored, Dr. Anbar stands and strides over to the Head of Security, as if the sweating, gasping hulk from a moment before was a mass hallucination. "Treadwell," said Dr. Anbar, with a nod.

"Doctor," said burly Treadwell, dipping his buzz cut in reply.

"What got me out of bed at this time of night?"

"There's a disturbance in the 'M' wing, doctor."

"Send some of your boys over there to straighten it out," said Dr. Anbar, as if he were addressing not only a subordinate, but an imbecile.

"I did that," Treadwell said, in much the same tone. "Four-man team, stun guns, and billy clubs, went out two hours ago and vanished."

"Vanished?"

The buzz cut nods. "So, I sent two more four-man teams to find the first team, and they haven't checked back in either. We have zero comm, A/V is down..."

Dr. Anbar interrupts with a wave and said, "In English, if you don't mind."

Treadwell takes a deep breath and said, "All lines of communication are down between us and the rest of the facility. The phones in this room work, and I can call out, but I can't call into the hospital." Dr. Anbar picks up a phone, dials a four-digit extension, and is rewarded with a fast, busy signal. "The audio and video surveillance system is down. I initiated a lockdown, and, if the board is correct, every door in the building is sealed with one exception."

"Which one?" asks Dr. Anbar, looking at a diagram of the entire mental facility on the wall and saw the one doorway flashing green, instead of glowing a steady red.

Treadwell shakes his head behind the doctor's back. "Which room do you think I would wake you up for?" No one knows exactly what goes on in that room, except Dr. Anbar. The doctor had made sure that all security cameras only show the corridors around the room, but not inside the room. This still offered security officers a clear view of the Head of Psychiatry's daily visits with crate upon crate of machine parts.

"Oh, that room," Dr. Anbar said, nodding while tapping the display with his pudgy finger, "In case of an incident with those patients, we are supposed to alert the FBI. Have you alerted them already?"

"They have a team in transit."

"Good," said Dr. Anbar, going down a shade in the color spectrum with sweat starting back up. "Good," he repeated. "It's good that you've notified them."

Dr. Anbar looks around the room and notices, for the first

time, that the twelve monitors on the wall are black. The date, time, and area name are still displayed in one corner, but no image was transmitted. "Is there any..." Dr. Anbar starts to say, his hand giving a vague wave at the wall.

"Surveillance footage before the incident? Yes, there is. It doesn't make much sense, but you can watch it."

"Actually, I was going to ask about coffee, but video before the incident would be good, too." Dr. Anbar sits in one of the security officer's chair, while the Treadwell goes to the coffeepot. "Black, six sugars, son."

Treadwell returns with the coffee and sits next to Dr. Anbar. The twelve monitors playback video from earlier in the day. "Everything was normal until the Feds dropped off two more patients."

CHAPTER FOUR

"Nar-Bak, the conveyance decelerates."

I nod in agreement, a habit I picked up from the locals. "Indeed, it does." My visual receptors are locked on the interior wall of the conveyance, my thinking membrane is to the brim with thoughts of dark origin. "They shall make us build another machine to print their Pictographs of Power," I whistle. "They are a species too greedy for their own good."

Glee-Tar doesn't whistle back a response.

"My performance as an elder is lacking, Glee-Tar. Contradict me not. My thinking membrane has processed this situation too many times with the same result for it to be otherwise." My whistle becomes the barest whisper. "If we survive this debacle of my doing and we gaze once again upon the planet of our fathers, you must report me. The Supreme Council must know my deficiencies. Though, I will be flayed and fed to the Jernicks, then the Jernicks will be crushed and burned, their remains launched into the farthest reaches of the great void. You must report me, or we will both perish because of my negligence." I look at Glee-Tar. His mouth is wide, as his tongue wiggles with happiness. "I expected you to be sad, although accepting of my final decision, as your elder. Are my skills as an elder so poor that the thought of my demise fills you with joyous rapture?"

"Your father's father is near at hand. Can you not sense the magnitude of his soul shadow, Nar-Bak?"

I start to whistle a contradiction, but then, even I can feel the weight of my father's father's soul shadow. My mind tastes the incandescence of his enlightenment, and I know that salvation from this disaster is nigh.

CHAPTER FIVE_

"Receiving takes custody of the transfers," said Treadwell, narrating for the Head of Psychiatry. "Then, the Feds leave, everyone has trouble controlling them. They keep trying to run off."

"Are you new?" Dr. Anbar asks. "Everyone tries to escape when they first arrive. Have you not worked *Receiving* before?"

Treadwell takes a deep breath. "That's the thing, doctor. They weren't trying to escape, they were trying to get *in*."

"What do you mean?"

"This is them running here," said Treadwell, pointing to a monitor, "away from the front gate. Then, my guards got them under control, got them through the next set of doors, but they run off again."

"What's going on in this one?" Dr. Anbar asks, pointing to a different monitor.

Treadwell rubs his neck, dreading the fallout from what he is about to admit. "The guards lost them, right before the crossroads, and had to call us to find them on the cameras."

All the cameras cycled through the corridors, until one found the new patients tugging on a door at the main hub of the facility. "Which door were they trying to open?" asks Dr. Anbar, ignoring Treadwell's statement about patients being alone in the facility.

"The door to the 'M' wing."

"How did they know where your men were taking them?"

"I have no idea."

CHAPTER SIX_

Glee-Tar and I run past the Aborigines' house-caves, drawn to my father's father's soul shadow like an An-Nait to a Nosaj pool. Our guides open the door for us. We are enveloped in the erotic bureaucracy of unfettered parliamentary procedures. The meeting pauses until the guides depart, and we're entombed in the house-cave with our kin and peers. As is the custom, we are ignored until the appropriate time.

"The sustenance that the natives feed us continues to lack flavonoids recognized as wholesome," Glee-Tar's sister's husband's brother whistles to those gathered for the meeting. "Though, determined by this exploratory committee," he said, waving his hand at the other two members of his committee, "continued assimilation of the contained nutrients..."

"In moderation," said one of the committee members.

"...in moderation, of course, will allow our continued survival on a physical level. Data are insufficient, at this time, to determine the impact of our spiritual wellbeing."

All present push this information psychically through their thought membranes. Once inducted and accepted, each member whistles acknowledgement and rub their forearms together.

My father's father annotated universal acceptance of this report, then cleared his sound tube. "Is there any further old business?" he asks, waiting a heartbeat and received no response. "Thus, this concludes old business. Is there any new business?"

Everyone turns their visual receptors toward Glee-Tar and me.

"Esteemed chair-being," I whistle, "I am in possession of new business."

"Scribe," my father's father whistles, "record the presence of Glee-Tar and Nar-Bak on the rolls, and annotate that they were not present at the beginning of the meeting, but under present circumstances, I move that their demerits for lack of punctuality be waived for this instance of insubordination. Do I have a second?"

"I second the motion," whistles an elder that I did not recognize.

"Motion carries," my father's father whistles. "Chair yields the floor to Nar-Bak."

I clear the nervous buildup of digestive juices from my speaking hole and whistle my report to the nine missing scouts. At the conclusion, the room fell silent, the sensory overload of nine, thinking membranes absorbed all the ambient sound.

Glee-Tar's sister's husband's brother whistles for clarification. "The Aboriginal love of the Pictographs of Power is well known," he said, "but this anti-evolution theory..." His whistle trails off, as others whistle their lack of understanding.

My father's father raises his pointing appendage and silences everyone's whistles. "How the natives achieved reverse evolution is immaterial. What is paramount is their lack of adequate defense."

One by one, Glee-Tar and I watch the data seep through the thinking membranes of each present scout. In unison, they rub their forearms together, their bifurcated tongues all waggle in joy at Glee-Tar and me.

"Chair moves to adjourn and signal the invasion fleet. Do I have a second?"

"I second the motion," Glee-Tar whistles.

"Motion carries. Ready the suit," my father's father whistles.

"Suit?" I ask.

The remaining eight scouts drag various machines to the center of the room.

"We've been busy, waiting for your arrival, grandson," whistles my father's father, as he tousles my hair.

"Grandfather," I whistle in dismay, "not in front of Glee-Tar."

"Your junior will think no less of you. Correct, Glee-Tar?"

"Most correct, most perspicacious elder," Glee-Tar whistles. "Where did you get all those machines?"

"The fat king of these caves gave us parts to print him Pictographs of Power," my father's father whistles.

"But there are enough parts to make a hundred machines," I whistle.

"He wants us to make him all sorts of machines. He probably intends to sell them for a different type of Pictographs of Power. His greed is unrivaled. I shall enjoy the subjugation of his species."

Glee-Tar nears the machines, his visual receptors soaking in each screw and nut. "Percipient elder?"

"Yes, Glee-Tar?"

"How does this device function?"

The other scouts cease their toiling and step away.

"First, it needs to be activated, so it can charge its energy storage cells. Then, we wait."

"How is it activated?"

"Just slap your grabbing appendages together twice, and it does the rest."

CHAPTER SEVEN_

"Once all the machines are in the center of the room," Treadwell said, "one of the new patients claps his hands, and the lights go out."

Dr. Anbar slams down his empty coffee cup and stands up. "This is ridiculous, Treadwell."

"Excuse me?"

"I can't believe *this* got me out of bed. I'm going down there."

"Doctor," Treadwell said, as he trails the Head of Psychiatry to the door, "twelve of my men have already gone there and haven't returned. We need to wait for the Feds to show up."

Dr. Anbar pokes his stubby finger into Treadwell's chest and said, "Then, perhaps you shouldn't have hired a bunch of cream puffs to work here. You're up for review."

Treadwell considered telling Dr. Anbar that most of his staff had seen combat in the military, but all that came out when he opened his mouth was, "Let me get the door for you, doctor."

Dr. Anbar storms through the facility, his weight and lack

of physical fitness forgotten in his rage. He notes that each cell in the hospital is locked, but the doorways between wings are wide open. "Dammit, Treadwell," said Dr. Anbar, mumbling to himself. "You bleed incompetence."

At the 'M' wing entrance, hallway lights provide a dim flicker, which slows the Head of Psychiatry's pace from a storm to a bare drizzle. He sneaks through the wing, stops outside the open cell door and presses himself against the wall. Realizing that Treadwell and his men can probably see him and laugh about the doctor sneaking through his own facility like a thief, he stands up straight, takes a deep breath, and steps into the cell to give these miscreants what-for.

"What is the meaning..." Dr. Anbar asks, as it's all he could get out before the giant robot in the center of the room grabs him by the throat and dangles him a foot off the ground.

Ten minutes after the doctor had stormed out, Treadwell lost his internal argument, forcing him to look for the fat bastard. He checks the clip in his pistol for the fifth time, as he walks alone through the hospital. He forbade any of his men to follow him. They were happy to oblige.

The doctor and patients are nowhere to be found in the 'M' wing. The twelve guards are asleep on the cell's floor. Not knocked unconscious, but simply asleep. Some are snoring. After the first three don't wake up to his shaking and shouting their names, he gives up and decides to see what's on the other side of the huge hole in the cell's wall.

On a little hill between the building and fence, he can see what looks like a robot dangling the doctor from its right hand. As he gets closer, he can see the patients' faces peering out at him. Two faces in each leg, one acting as the shin, one as the thigh. Same thing in the arms, one in the bicep, one in the forearm. Two in the chest, one for each lung, he reckons. The head seems partially empty. Then, he remembers that there was an odd number of them. The exoskeleton was built for an even dozen, but someone didn't show up.

"Stop where you are," said a voice, booming from the robot.

Treadwell froze, his pistol aimed at the ground in front of his feet.

"You can understand me?" asks the robot.

"Yes, I can understand you," said Treadwell.

"Oh good. We were afraid that the translation software wouldn't function properly." Then, a series of loud whistles come from the speaker.

"What was that?" asks Treadwell, after he uncovers his ears.

"I was merely congratulating the team that built the translator."

Treadwell assumes the oldest patient in the head compartment is doing the talking, but he isn't sure.

Dr. Anbar tries to speak around the hand holding his throat, but all that comes out is a strangled approximation, "Treadwell!"

"I can't let you kill the doctor," said Treadwell, as he thumbs the hammer back on his pistol. "You can go about your business, but I won't allow you to kill that man."

"Kill him?" asks the booming voice. "Your fat king will live a long and prosperous life, as the pet of our prime elder."

Treadwell eases the hammer forward on his sidearm and holsters it. "As long as you aren't going to kill him."

"Treadwell," said the doctor, hissing but everyone ignored him.

"So, now what? The Feds are on their way. They won't let you go."

"Our conveyance is imminent."

Treadwell nods, not knowing what that meant, but it was a nice night.

"I'm not sure how I'm going to explain all this," Treadwell said.

"You are the prophet of the coming invasion. Tell your world that we will return. Now, we must be going. Enjoy what remains of your life."

The robot's available hand flexes once, twice, three times. A beam of light pierces the clouds and burns a hole in the grass, just out of the robot's reach. The robot sidesteps and the machine hand wraps around the stationary lightning bolt. Once its grip is secure, the robot, with Dr. Anbar in its other hand, is shot up the beam into the night's sky.

Treadwell stares at the black spot in the hill, once his night vision returns. The air is thick with the smell of burning grass. He decides that now is as good a time as any to use up his sick days. Once his shift is over, of course.

THE END

THE FORTRESS OF EVIL

FORTRESS OF EVIL_

The Continuing Adventures of **Agent Maxwell, Intergalactic Security Agency.**

The last we knew, our intrepid hero, Agent Maxwell, had scaled the sheer walls of Mount Anger with his platoon of Space Marines borrowed from his old friend, General "Skip" Tracer. At the summit, the henchmen of Professor Achbad had opened fire from the safety of the parapets surrounding the nearly completed Fortress of Evil, pinning down Maxwell and his Space Marines. When all hope seemed lost, Mark Four, Maxwell's artificially intelligent phaser pistol, showed Maxwell how to build an improvised trebuchet out of the debris at hand. Medieval siege weapon built, fortress gates breached, Maxwell led his Space Marines into the labyrinthine innards of the Fortress of Evil.

The booby-trapped maze of tunnels and hallways claimed most of the Space Marines within moments of their entrance. Hopelessly lost, Maxwell was left with trusty Mark Four and Private Bill from Nebraska.

. . .

"I've got a bad feeling about this, sir," said Private Bill, snuffling.

Maxwell relights his cigar using Mark Four's flame-thrower feature. "Nothing to worry about, Private. I've been in hairier situations than this cooking my breakfast," said Maxwell, as he turns to buck up the Marine a bit more, but no one's there. "Damn booby-traps. I guess it's just you and me from here on out, Mark Four."

"Ready when you are, Max," replies the pistol.

Maxwell thought to himself, *Even the electronic voice coming from my pistol seems to doubt me.*

The muscular agent stops at an intersection, his big paw of a hand rubs the stubble on his chin, as he looks at his options.

Left, right, forward, they all look the same as where I just came from. How am I supposed to do this now? I'm too old for this crap. They've got guys at the Academy with computers implanted in the side of their skulls for God's sake.

"What do you think, Mark Four?" asks Maxwell.

"According to my calculations," said Mark Four, "to be precise, we're not going in circles yet, if that is what you want to know."

"Thanks," Maxwell said, grumbling.

Computers in their skulls. All I've got is a talking pistol with no sense of direction and a creaky set of knees.

"I'm going to head this way. Keep your sensors peeled for any sort of trouble."

"Max?" asks Mark Four.

"Yep," said Maxwell, through his stogie, while creeping down the corridor.

"I'm picking up some sort of chemical in the air..." said Mark Four.

Suddenly, everything went black for Maxwell.

. . .

"Open your eyes, Agent Maxwell."

Maxwell had been taking in his surroundings, feigning sleep, to see if he could figure out where he was being held.

"No use pretending."

This guy is good.

"Seriously," said the voice, "I mean, you talk in your sleep and that stopped like five minutes ago, and then, the fake snoring started. So, open your eyes already."

Damn.

Being bound to the table was old news. Maxwell wasn't going to do the amateur-night routine of, *I'm going to flail around and act shocked that I'm tied up.* Instead, Maxwell rolls his head to the side the voice was coming from and opened his eyes. "Let me go now," Maxwell said, "and this will go a lot easier for you."

"Ooh, scary," said the man on a skull-shaped throne, waving his hands in mock horror. "I bet you were a force to be reckoned with before color television. But no, I think I'll leave you tied up, and things will get much worse for you. How's that sound?"

"Have we met before?" asks Maxwell.

"Impossible," said the man on the throne. Sweeping his robes back with a flourish, he came closer to the immobilized ISA super-agent.

"It's just that your goatee and cape with the Lucky Charms marshmallow shapes, it's all very familiar," said Maxwell.

"Marshmallow shapes? These are powerful runic symbols," said the man, gathering a corner of his cape and thrusting it at Maxwell. "This is the Ankh of Temorah. Name one cereal that has Ankh of Temorah marshmallows in it."

Maxwell shakes his head.

"You can't, can you? That's because carnivorous leopard beetles the size of dinner plates would rain from the sky and devour everyone in sight," said the caped man.

"Right," Maxwell said.

"They would, I've seen it."

"If that's true, why isn't there a thunderstorm of beetles wherever you walk?" asks Maxwell.

"It's because, on this side, I have..." said the man, grabbing the other corner of his cape, then looked at Maxwell. "I don't have to explain this to you." He smooths out his robe and hangs his head. "You are messing up the speech I prepared, and I don't appreciate it."

"Oh, my mistake. I thought this was the chat before you torture me, not the diabolical monologue," Maxwell said. "Carry on, by all means, carry on."

"Thank you," said the caped man, giving a slight bow. "Where was I? Welcome to the Fortress of Evil, Agent Maxwell, nice of you to *drop in*." The caped man pauses and looks around. "Sorry, there's supposed to be ominous music there." Pausing again, the caped man takes a deep breath and said, "FORTRESS OF EVIL...FORTRESS OF EVIL...must be broken, again."

"I don't get it," said Maxwell.

"Ominous music? After saying, 'Fortress of Evil,' a pipe organ should go, 'dun-dun-DUN.'"

"No, the *'drop in'* thing,"

"You fell through a trap door. *Drop in.* What's not to get?"

"I lost consciousness and woke up here. I don't remember any trap door."

Producing a notebook from under his cape, the man scribbles a note. "We keep losing pressure on the knockout gas. The contractor was told there was a leak. Sorry, you were supposed to fall through a trap door, *then* get gassed in the holding cell. Just a matter of style. Anyway," said the caped man, clearing his throat and raising his arms, "...BUT YOU ARE TOO LATE MAXWELL. SOON THE FORTRESS OF EVIL WILL BE COMPLETE, AND THE MASTER OF DARKNESS WILL RISE. I, PROFESSOR ACHBAD, LORD OF EVIL, WILL CONQUER THIS SOLAR SYSTEM."

"Excuse me," said Maxwell, "I don't mean to interrupt, but can I just say something?"

"Certainly, this is the first time I've given the speech. I'd appreciate your feedback," said Professor Achbad, hovering a pen over his notebook.

"First of all, 'this solar system' is aiming kind of low, just my opinion. If you're going to summon the Master of Darkness, you might as well go whole hog and conquer the galaxy."

Professor Achbad nods. "Good point, good point," he said, mumbling as he writes, "Conquer galaxy, not solar system. Anything else?"

"You seem kind of new to all this, and the attrition rate is really high for your job, I get that. If the first time goes bad, there usually isn't a second time, know what I mean?"

"Of course," said Professor Achbad.

"I've seen people summon the Master of Darkness before, and not to rain brimstone on your parade, but he doesn't really play well with others."

"What do you mean?"

"I've seen the MOD destroy everything within four parsecs, and the first thing he always destroys, always, is the person who summoned him," said Maxwell.

"Really? Why?"

"Well, I'm not positive, but I think that since you summoned him, he knows that you're the only one within earshot with the ability to dismiss him. If you're out of the way, he can run amuck until one of our crews shows up and sends him back to The Pit."

"Ooh, that sets up the next part of my speech," said Professor Achbad, putting his notebook back, under his cape. "Maxwell, tell me it will never work."

Maxwell rolls his eyes and said, "Whatever. It will never work, Achbad."

Professor Achbad raises his arms over his head. "THAT'S WHERE YOU'RE WRONG, MAXWELL. THIS FORTRESS IS SITUATED ON THE APEX OF MOUNT ANGER AND THIS VERY ROOM IS 666 METERS FROM SEA LEVEL. EACH WALL IS AT A PRECISE ANGLE OF 66.6 DEGREES FROM ONE OF THE SIX MERIDIANS OF POWER. WHEN THE MAIN DOORS OPEN TOMORROW, THE SIXTH LUNAR CYCLE BEGINS. ALL SIX MOONS WILL FORM A PERFECT PENTAGRAM IN THE NIGHT SKY, THE WIND WILL REACH 666 MILES AN HOUR AND THE HARMONICS AS IT TRAVELS THROUGH THE UPPER HALLWAYS WILL SUMMON THE MASTER OF DARKNESS FROM THE PIT BENEATH YOU," said Professor Achbad, dropping his arms. "What? I can see that face you're making. Say something smart. Just say it."

"Not to nit-pick, but don't you think you need to pick a standard of measurement?" asks Maxwell.

"What?"

"You just said 'meters from sea level,' then 'miles per hour.' You really should be all the way metric or all the way standard," said Maxwell.

"It doesn't work if I do it in just metrics. Six-hundred-sixty-six miles an hour is like..."

"A thousand seventy-one kilometers."

"Get it? There's nothing nefarious about 1,071."

"Maybe you're reaching, is all I'm saying. It's like those conspiracy people who still think we haven't landed on the moon."

"I hate those people," Professor Achbad said. "Don't you have a base there?"

"It's more like a staging area on the dark side, it's not a full-on base. But, yes."

"I get your point. But this is the closest I could come, and it was cheap," Professor Achbad said. "You saw what it looks like outside, the realtor practically gave it away. They dropped the selling price because of the Hell-Bat infestation, and I'm trying to work them into my theme. Do you know how hard it is to get rid of Hell-Bats?"

"Not really my specialty," Maxwell said, looking around the room for holding cells but didn't see any. "Where are the Space Marines? You didn't go and straight up kill them, did you?"

Professor Achbad waves his hands in the air and said, "No, of course not. This might be my first attempt at dominating the solar system, but I do know a thing or two." The eyes on Professor Achbad's platinum skull medallion lit up red and a Vincent Price maniacal laugh comes from the same area. "Excuse me, for one minute."

"Certainly."

Professor Achbad flips open the skull and places it to his ear. "PROFESSOR ACHBAD, LORD OF EVIL, MASTER OF...yes, this is Mike...I'm fine, how are you? Good. What can I do for you? Really? No one ever mentioned anything about a handicap-accessible bathroom. Yes, it is zoned commercial, but...yes, I am in the fortress right now...by all means...I'm in the holding room below the sacrifice chamber. See you in a minute. Ta-ta," said Professor Achbad, snapping the skull phone shut and turning back to Maxwell. "Sorry about that. One of the contractors has some questions. Where were we?"

"You said on the phone that your first name is Mike. You're not Mike Moriarty Jr., by any chance? If you are, I battled your father a couple times," said Maxwell.

"My father wasn't in the business. You probably battled my grandfather. I'm Mike Moriarty the Third."

"Are you sure it wasn't your father? It wasn't that long ago."

"I'm sure it wasn't my father. He's the black sheep of the family. He prepares taxes," said Professor Achbad, spatting his words, "at H&R Block."

"But Mike Moriarty was your age when I battled him, and I'm not that old," said Maxwell.

Professor Achbad clears his throat and rolls his eyes.

"What?" Maxwell demands.

"Well, I don't want to be telling tales out of school, but have you ever had an *unsuccessful* mission?"

"No," said Maxwell with a snort, "of course not. I'm the best-trained agent the ISA has ever seen. Why? What do you know?"

"You don't spend much time on BluTube, do you?"

"I'm working all the time. I don't have time to lurk around on the Web," said Maxwell.

"I'm sorry to be the one that tells you this, but every time you get killed on a mission, ISA just clones you, again. You don't remember the failed missions because ISA doesn't have the brain with those memories to reload into your new body. There's an online blooper reel of you getting greased, like a hundred different ways."

"I'm a clone?" asks Maxwell.

"It's really quite funny."

"I'm a clone?"

"Paul Simon's *50 Ways to Leave Your Lover* plays in the

background. I nearly pissed my robes the first time I saw it. The Order of Evil, Mayhem, and Chaos plays it every year at its annual banquet."

"I'm a clone?" said Maxwell, still in shock.

"Yes, yes, you're a clone. Gads, what a baby. Ah, yes, the plumbers are here," said Professor Achbad, as the pipe organ activates and ominous music blares from hidden speakers. The two plumbers walk into the room. "Really?" Professor Achbad asks, looking at the ceiling, "ominous music for the plumbers," said Professor Achbad, as the ominous music repeats, "but nothing for Professor Achbad or Fortress of Evil?" Professor Achbad waits for a moment and said. "I'm going to kill that Muzak installer."

The younger of the two plumbers walk past Professor Achbad and plops into the skull throne. "Excuse me, but that's my throne," said Professor Achbad to the elder plumber. "He can't sit on my throne."

The elder plumber cocks his baseball hat with the A.O. Smith Water Heater logo back on his head and moves a cigarette from one side of his mouth to the other, using his teeth. "Between you and me, I wouldn't ask him to move. He hasn't been having a very good day, and he stepped in something on the way here."

"Probably Hell-Bat guano," said Professor Achbad, nodding. The younger plumber pulls a flat-head screwdriver from his cargo pants pocket to dig the infernal fundament from his sole. Professor Achbad returns his attention to the elder plumber to ask, "What news? Will my fortress be ready for the start of the sixth lunar cycle?"

"When does that start again?" asks the elder plumber, unfurling a blueprint across Maxwell's bound legs.

"Tomorrow."

"Tomorrow!" said the younger plumber.

"Matt," said the elder plumber, pointing with his cigarette, "what did we discuss in the truck?"

"I know, I know. I talk to you, you talk to the customers," said the younger plumber, without looking up from the bottom of his boot.

"Sorry, doctor..."

"It's professor, actually, Professor Achbad."

"Sorry, professor. Little family thing, you understand."

"You two are related?"

"I forgot that we haven't officially met. That's my son, Matt, and I'm Jack," said Jack, extending his hand and Professor Achbad shakes it, "of Jack and Sons Plumbing." The pipe organ kicks on again.

Without releasing Jack's hand, Professor Achbad produces a dagger, flings it over Matt's shoulder, and the nearest speaker dies in mid, '...dun...' "A family business, excellent. I took this over from my grandfather. I'm a huge supporter of small businesses."

"Good, glad to hear it," said Jack, extricating his hand from Professor Achbad's grasp.

"Sons? Is there another one running around?"

"My oldest son doesn't work for me anymore. Hurt his back in the Space Marines. He's in optics now."

"Death-rays? That sort of thing?" asks Professor Achbad, rubbing his palms together.

"Prescription glasses, actually."

Professor Achbad cackles maniacally. "Even better," he said, "I have a pair of sunglasses where the nosepiece fell off, some old Ray-Bans that I've had since the dawn of time. Do you think he can fix that?"

"I'm sure he can. He's in the new mall that opened a few months ago, just off the highway."

"By the cell phone store?"

Jack nods.

"Superb. I'll have one of my minions take the glasses to him when they get me a car charger for this thing," said Professor Achbad, pointing at the skull phone around his neck. "But you came here with grave news." Professor Achbad raises his hands to the sky. "Spare not a single detail."

"Maybe it would be easier, if I just show you," said Jack, rolling up the blueprint and tucking it under his arm. "Matt?"

"I gotta get this shit off my boots."

Jack shrugs and said, "We'll just come back for him. First, we should look at the drainage in the sacrifice chamber."

Professor Achbad follows the elder plumber into the corridor, their voices fade as they walk. "I thought there was a floor drain up there?"

"There is, but because of the amount of magma that you're going to be pumping in from the underworld, you're going to need at least three more," said Jack.

Once Professor Achbad's voice can no longer be heard, Maxwell said, "Hey, kid, cut me loose."

The younger plumber still on Professor Achbad's throne, looks at Maxwell and arches an eyebrow and asks Maxwell, "Who? Me?"

"Cut me loose before they come back," said Maxwell.

"Dude, I'm like 28. I don't answer to, 'kid.'" said Matt, bending back to the tread on his boots.

Maxwell takes a deep breath and said, "I'm Agent Maxwell with the Intergalactic Security Agency. I'm trying to stop Professor Achbad, before he can complete this temple and unleash the Master of Darkness on this solar system. And you're sitting there, scraping bat crap off your shoes."

"How exactly is Professor Achbad going to take over the solar system?" asks Matt, more interested in the bottom of his boots than anything Maxwell has to say.

"When he opens the doors upstairs, the wind going through the specifically aligned walls will create a tone that will open the seal on The Pit."

"And when's this all supposed to happen?" asks Matt, still not looking up.

"The sixth lunar cycle starts tomorrow."

Matt laughs. "This place isn't going to be finished by tomorrow, not even a week from tomorrow. We still need a plumbing inspection before we can get the Certificate of Occupancy, and that won't be anytime soon."

"Why not?" asks Maxwell.

Matt looks in the corridor, then walks over to Maxwell. "Are you and Professor Achbad partners or something?"

"Absolutely not. I would never join forces with him," said Maxwell.

"That's not the kind of partners I am talking about."

Maxwell looks down at his restraints and said, "What? No, I'm not into that sort of thing. Not that there's anything wrong with that sort of thing. ISA is all about inclusivity. Professor Achbad is potentially my arch-nemesis."

"Alright, between you and me," said Matt, looking down the hallway again and lowering his voice, "this guy should have been cracking the whip on the cement guys and electricians. They took forever. We put in a bid for this job like three years ago, and then they hired some other plumber. He got about half of it finished, then disappeared. No one knows where he went, so we got the job. Now, it's on us if Professor Achbad misses the lunar cycle or whatever. Dude wanted us here two weeks ago, but we were finishing up the Fortress of Impervitude on Hella-13, and those guys are in the same club or whatever. It's bullshit."

"What guys?" Maxwell asks.

Matt shrugs. "Professor Achbad and Lord Four Quarter or whatever."

"Lord Fuqua?"

"Something like that."

"You've been to Lord Fuqua's new base?"

"Is there an echo in here? Yeah, what did I just say?"

"But how? It's the Fortress of Impervitude."

"From the front," said Matt, shaking his head, "You can't get on the planet from the front, let alone into the fortress. But there's a service entrance big enough for us to drive our truck into."

"Where?" Maxwell asks.

"Corner of First Street and Highway 85 in Ault."

"Ault? I've never been to that planet," said Maxwell.

"It's not a planet, it's a small farm town in Colorado. In the United States, you know?"

"You have to release me," I said, struggling with my restraints with no results. "This information will prove invaluable to ISA."

"Man, I'm not jeopardizing us getting another job by cutting you lose. Sorry."

"But your brother was a Space Marine."

"Sorry, bro," said Matt, dropping onto the throne, again. "There are way too many plumbers and not enough work at this end of the universe. Besides, nothing's going to happen tomorrow. We're going to have to move at least two walls to get the drainage in. Then, the walls won't be at the precise angle that dude wants. So, just relax. I'm sure they'll send reinforcements for you."

Maxwell stares at the ceiling, knowing they aren't sending reinforcements. They'll just let me die again and respawn me at headquarters. Then, a thought strikes. "Sorry to bother you again, but is there a drawer in the armrest of that throne?"

Matt looks in one armrest, then the other and said, "Yeah, it looks like it."

"I'm sure that he said something about a television in here, do you mind?"

Matt roots around and comes out holding Mark Four. "Is this supposed to be a remote?"

"Mark Four, cut me loose," Maxwell shouts.

"Righty-o, Max," said Mark Four, as the phaser pistol, bucking in the younger plumber's hand, melts Maxwell's bindings.

Able to stand, Maxwell rolls his big shoulders back and pop his neck. Maxwell takes Mark Four out of Matt's hand and with a flourish, holsters the pistol. "Thanks, citizen."

"That's messed up, man," said Matt. "You're going to get us fired."

"I'm going to shut this guy down," I said. "You coming with me?"

Matt shrugs and follows the agent into the corridor. About 20 yards in, Matt grabs Maxwell's shoulder. "Booby-trap," Matt said, pointing at the floor. "I'll lead, just pay attention to where I step."

Five uneventful minutes later, they hear Professor Achbad and Jack.

"Really?" asks Professor Achbad, "You need that much room between the edge of the toilet and the wall? I had no idea."

"And another thing, if you're only going to have one urinal, it has to be handicap accessible. So, we need to lower this one by about a foot," Jack said, as Maxwell sneaks around the corner, Mark Four in his hand. Matt walks in, back straight, hands in pockets, and shakes his head at Jack.

"A foot closer to the floor? People might as well be using the floor drain, if it's that low," Professor Achbad said, his back to the door.

Maxwell spins Professor Achbad around. Terror registers in the villain's eyes, until the butt of Mark Four connects with his forehead, forcing Professor Achbad to crumple to the floor with a high-pitched squeak. Maxwell bites the end off a fresh cigar and spits it out.

"Where's the prison in this monstrosity?" asks Maxwell, hoisting Professor Achbad over his shoulder.

Jack jerks his thumb toward the hallway, then points at Matt and said, "Did you...?"

"Hey, I didn't do anything," said Matt. "He got himself loose, as far as I'm concerned. Did you deposit Achbad's check, yet?"

"Yesterday," Jack said.

"Good," said Matt, as they follow Maxwell carrying Professor Achbad out of the public restroom.

The plumbers round the corner to the prison level and watch Maxwell melt the cell door controls with Mark Four's laser.

"You could have just hit the button marked, 'OPEN,'" said Matt.

Space Marines swarm Maxwell with a cheer, then take Professor Achbad and bind him with rappelling rope. "Get General Tracer on the horn, Corporal. Tell him this base now belongs to ISA."

"Aye, aye, sir," said the Corporal, with a salute.

"Really?" Matt asks, "It's ISA's property now?"

"That's right, plumbers." Ominous music plays. "I'm claiming this fortress in the name of the Intergalactic Security Agency."

"In that case," Jack said, cigarette clenched between his teeth, "we'll overlook the fact that you didn't provide us hard hats or hearing protection as required by OSHA on all government structures. And you're going to need to get the carpenters and flooring guys back here, or you'll have a major lawsuit on your hands."

"Yeah," said Matt, chiming in, "handicap accessible is one thing in a commercial building, but 'no-step' handicap accessible in a government building is a whole new ballgame."

Jack unrolls the blueprint on a table and takes out a pencil. Matt joins him, as they pour over the schematic, marking changes.

"Sir," said Private Bill from Nebraska, whispering to Maxwell, "me and some of the boys could rough those two fellers up and leave them down here with Professor Achbad."

"Thanks, Private, but that's the last thing we need, right now. They're union. You ever dealt with the Pipefitter's Union? Scary stuff," Maxwell said, while Private Bill shakes his head. "It ain't pretty, let me tell you. Do you hear something?"

"Look out," a Space Marine shouts.

Maxwell spins toward the door, Mark Four drawn. A ten-foot-tall stone wheel catches him in the chest and flattens Maxwell against the prison's wall. Mark Four falls from his limp hands.

"Corporal," said Private Bill from Nebraska, "tell General Tracer that the Fortress of Evil is ours, but we're gonna need a new Agent Maxwell."

If you enjoyed *Leonard* or any of the other stories you've just read, I'd like to recommend my full-length, dystopian, science fiction novel *L.I.F.E. in the 23rd Century*.

It's 1984 if it were written by Monty Python. Not as dark as *Brazil*, not as absurd as "The Fish-Slapping Dance."

Or to put it another way: fake news, a wall around America, inept billionaire politicians, sedated populace working meaningless jobs to the benefit of no one but their corporate overlords. But also flying cars and getting a cavity search when you clock in for work everyday.

A humorous, dystopian future world to distract you from whatever dystopian nightmare you may be living in.

Turn the page for a sample.

L.I.F.E. IN THE 23RD CENTURY — AN EXCERPT_

A DYSTOPIAN TALE OF CONSUMERISM, CORPORATE COFFEE, AND CROW BARS

"A comfortable, smooth, reasonable, democratic unfreedom prevails in advanced industrial civilization, a token of technical progress. Indeed, what could be more rational than the suppression of individuality in the mechanization of socially necessary but painful performances..." — Herbert Marcuse

This is *not* a public service announcement.

Repeat, this is **not** a public service announcement, nor a threat-level upgrade.

An unidentified terrorist cell has not, repeat, not leveled the corner store with explosives made from easily attained household products.

Your life is not in danger.

You should not make your way in an orderly fashion—being mindful of children, the elderly, and the infirm—to the hardened concrete bunker in the basement of your apartment building. Prayers for protection sent up to the deity of your choice will go unheeded for numerous reasons; especially because they are unnecessary.

This is not the Emergency Broadcast System.

This is not even a test of the Emergency Broadcast System, which, in this instance, is not the same as saying that this is a real emergency. Had this been an actual emergency, you would have been instructed in what to do. But you won't, because this isn't.

The head of Homeland Security will not issue a statement regarding the current situation. Swift Terror Assessment and Response teams will not be deployed to the scene. The Inquisitor Branch of Homeland Security will not launch a full-scale investigation into the incident.

There is no smoking crater to examine. No toppled building. No next of kin to notify. No one saying, "Is this your son/daughter/father/mother/brother/sister? We know it's hard, but we need to be sure, ma'am/sir."

Celebrities will not stage a telethon for the victims' families. Waiters will not ask you to donate toward building a memorial statue/reflecting pool/amusement park. Magnetic remembrance paraphernalia for your automobile will not be available at this store or any other patriotic retailer.

Suspected terrorists, accomplices of suspected terrorists, and all their relatives will not be shown wearing black hoods on every channel, while being led into a super-maximum federal detention center. Images of armed guards and thirty-foot electrified fences topped with razor wire around a squat building capable of withstanding ground zero nuclear assault will not be available for your viewing pleasure.

The President will not interrupt your must-watch, can't-miss sitcom. He will not give his rousing, "situation normal, there is nothing to fear" speech from the safety of Air Force One six miles above your apartment. He will neither plead with you to remain calm, nor assure you that everything is fine, while members of Congress are ferried to an impregnable bunker inside a mountain until the dust settles.

Doomsayers *will* say that this is an apocalyptic event. *The End of Days*.

Religious fanatics—ours and theirs—are like the lottery. Sooner or later, someone will get the numbers right.

However, at this moment, all apocalyptic seals remain unbroken. The Choir Invisible is still rehearsing for the grand finale. The Horsemen are doing nothing more terrible than letting their mounts graze.

There is no threat.

No attack.

No telethon.

No Apocalypse.
No terrorists.
Not tonight.
NO TERRORISTS.
Not tomorrow, either.
Trust me.

This has *not* been a public service announcement. We now return to **my** life, already in progress.

L.I.F.E.

Noun
: an electronic machine implanted in citizens of the United States of America starting in the 23rd century.

Abbreviation for:
Life-force Input and Feedback Equipment

CHAPTER ONE_

This sort of thing does not happen. Manufacturers install fail-safes, politicians enact laws against the possibility of the giant box rolling toward me. The box is two lanes wide, double the height of my car, and spins chunks of asphalt into the air when a corner hits the road. Except for me, the highway is clear, my car's auto-drive rocketing me closer and closer to the corrugated steel container. Collision-avoidance software warns me of the imminent impact. Surely, there must be some program built into my car, and at the last instant, my car will swerve to safety. The car is calculating. Sizing up the box. Waiting for the precise moment. I keep my hands in my lap, watching the box spin closer and closer, chunks of pavement bouncing off my car's windshield. The last thing I want to do is touch the steering wheel, engage manual drive, and nullify all the processing the car requires to save me.

The container takes to the air, and I see nothing but clear road in front of me. I knew there had to be something that would keep me safe.

A shadow falls across my car.

Then, the sun goes out, and everything stops.

Is that the last thing you remember?

The thought comes into my head, partly as a voice, partly as text.

Yes, I reply in my head.

What do you remember before that?

Before that?

Before that?

I was at work.

No, I was leaving work, I believe.

Yes, I was in the parking lot at work. The lasers in each eyelid painted a new message icon on my eyes, as I neared my car. Using the trackball in the roof of my mouth, I scrolled over with my tongue and selected the icon from the heads-up display; the message played.

Greetings, P. McGewan-X04.

I tried to see my car through the spectral image playing on my eye.

Today's audit is sponsored by the Office of Homeland Security and will help to ensure proper levels of patriotism throughout these United States. Please make your way to your vehicle with haste and have a nice day. God bless you. The soft-spoken woman disappears. The lasers paint a green glow around my car, just when I thought my vehicle location Gizmo needed to be updated, again.

The Auditor stands at my car's bumper, waiting. His Sanitary Human Interface Terminal circles in a lazy holding pattern over his head, like an indifferent vulture. When I stop at the prescribed six paces from him, the flat screen breaks from its holding pattern and approaches me. The Auditor didn't speak, didn't even turn to look at me. The Interface Terminal hovers a foot from the tip of my nose. A recording of the Auditor appears on the screen. I can see the actual, real-time Auditor punching commands into his wrist.

"Is this your conveyance, citizen?" barks the face on the screen, while the actual Auditor stares at the horizon, his face placid.

"Yes, sir." I click the button in the roof of my mouth, activating the heads-up display, and tongue the trackball of the mouth-mouse until I got to my car's title and registration. The documents display on the screen on my left wrist for the Auditor. The Terminal scans the title's barcode, and then the license plate.

By far, this was the easiest of Patriotism Audits. No historical trivia questions, no physical activity, no Bible verses to recite—just document production. Next, the face on the screen asks me about the magnetic memorabilia, and I'm already scrolling to those receipts.

"How many pieces of magnetic memorabilia are you displaying?"

"Seven, sir." I pull up the receipts on my wrist and hold them out for the Terminal's laser scanner. Once each magnet is scanned, I should be on my way.

"Why seven, citizen?"

The flesh-and-blood Auditor still does not glance in my direction, but his recorded face on the screen never breaks eye contact.

This is a new question.

"Four is the minimum required by law, but seven is suspicious. What are you hiding, citizen?"

Patriotism Rehab Prison, here I come. I swallow and try to think of an answer.

"And this one," a laser point jumps out of the Terminal and details a spot on one of the magnets, "is worn and discolored on the edge. Do you not respect the memory of the lives lost that this magnet commemorates?"

Your heartbeat is elevated, and you are perspiring. Would

you enjoy a mood stabilizer? Perhaps a muscle relaxant? Your personal counselor is only a tongue-click away.

I tongue-click, No, to all these on my heads-up display and try to think of a suitable answer for the Auditor.

"You are hereby charged with conduct unbecoming a Patriot and inappropriate commemoration of lives lost in the War on Terror. Fine of thirty-thousand credits or one year in Patriot Rehabilitation. How would you like to pay for society for your negligence, citizen?"

A charge sheet appears on my heads-up with my bank account next to it. Without looking over my shoulder, I knew a pair of Homies was standing by to drag me away, if I didn't choose the fine. As soon as the hourglass turns back to a pointer, I select the fine and watch the credits disappear.

The Homies slump off with the Auditor in trail, but his Terminal remains for a moment. "A Patriot remembers," whispers the face before following its master.

I peel the offensive magnet off the bumper. Dozens of my coworkers are being led to the hover buses that take them to Patriotism Rehab. Tuesday will be rough, like always. The rest of us, those who get to go home tonight, will have to pick up the slack for the missing coworkers, until they were rehabilitated or replaced.

As I turn, a glint of silver catches my eye. At the distant corner of the lot, where the Auditors head, stands the sole Inquisitor to rule them all. He's easy to spot. His obligatory black leather trench coat shapes his body into a perfect rectangle. His bald head pivots, his mirrored sunglasses reflect the sunlight, like twin searchlights of a malicious lighthouse. Watchful, patient, he waits for the next soul to splinter on his reef. For a moment and from a safe distance, the Inquisitor seemed ridiculous. He looks like an upside-down exclamation mark in front of the handful of contraband Spanish curse words that I know. Then, his gaze turns toward me, and I hustle to my car; auto-drive takes me away as soon as the door closes.

Very good. What happened before that?

The workday ended. It was Monday. Monday meant audits.

Even with twelve chipper reminders on the hour, every hour throughout the workday that Auditors would be coming, we still groaned as a collective when we saw them standing in the parking lot. The groan, per individual, equaled only a bare whisper, but multiplied by a thousand souls, it might as well have been a scream.

Patriots do not groan out loud at the sight of Auditors. Patriots look forward to proving their patriotism through weekly audits.

But there's still the groan. The groan that said, *Really? Again? Couldn't you pack it in for one week? Just one?*

The entire day shift dismounts the slidewalk and make their way through the lot. Not too slow. Not too fast. Patriots neither try to outrun Auditors, nor do they 'lollygag' which is the retro buzzword of the week. Last week, Patriots did not 'dilly-dally.'

The result of this unhurried rush looks like a drunken tornado. No one wants to lead; no one wants to bring up the rear. Everyone wants to be in the center. No one can see the whole group, no one can agree on the eye of the storm.

Coworkers parked closest to the building are met by Fitness Enforcement Agency Auditors, who always move the quickest due to their lack of auditing tools and body fat. The tan, muscular, and lightly oiled women in their bulletproof sports bras and spandex short-shorts go to work, shouting for squat thrusts.

"Jumping jacks, now move."

"On your back for Hello Dollies."

"On your feet, citizen. Run in place."

The rest of the lot is peppered with random Auditors from all branches of government. Besides FEA Auditors, the others use identical Terminals, and the only way to tell what sort of audit was to listen to the questions from the hovering screen. A Patriot knew every answer to every question that an Auditor might ask, but a smart Patriot eavesdropped, just in case they are asked the same questions in their audit.

"What is the Third Commandment?" shouts the face on the screen, while the thin strip of an Auditor checks her makeup in the mirror Gizmo on her L.I.F.E.

"Thou shalt have no other Gods before me," the citizen mumbles.

"Is that a question or a statement?" screams the Terminal.

"A statement, ma'am," said the citizen, this time louder and with more conviction, "thou shalt have no other Gods before me."

"Very good," said the Terminal. "Let's find out how well you know the Nicene Creed."

"What is the Seventeenth Amendment?" asks the next Auditor to a citizen standing at attention beside his vehicle.

"Congress shall have power to lay and collect taxes on incomes," the citizen said proudly to the screen, "from whatever source derived, without apportionment among the States, and without regard to any census or enumeration, sir."

"Very good," said the Patriotic History Auditor.

"Thank you, sir."

"Unfortunately, that's the Sixteenth Amendment," the disembodied head snaps, while the Auditor updates his status on his L.I.F.E. Two Homeland Security officers step up and grab the citizen. One Homie holds a gun to the citizen's head, while the other puts him in handcuffs.

"Wait," shouts the citizen, hands secured behind his back, "I know it. It's the Terms for Senators. I can recite it. Please, let me recite it." One of the Homies hits the citizen in the neck with a stun gun. The citizen turns silent and limp, as the Homies drag him away.

The pack of employees thins, as we progress. I had parked at the far end of the lot, not the last car in the lot—that would be suspicious—but close to the last car.

Where do you work, citizen?

United States Cubicles.

What do you do at United States Cubicles, citizen?

I ensure quality standards are met when the production line machinery installs drawer pulls.

What is your name, citizen?

P. McGewan-X04, cubicle production tech, fifth class.

Standby. Stimulant dispensing.

My awareness deepened by a small increment, as if I had transitioned from a vivid dream to a very drunken state of consciousness. The difference was subtle, but noticeable. For a moment, I believed I was still in a dream state, floating weightless. Or, I was dead. As I regain awareness, I noticed that my lips are stretched into an 'O' and a tube is taking up most of my mouth, headed down my throat.

I am neither dead, nor dreaming. I am in a hospital. More specifically, I am floating in the thick gel of a sensory-deprivation tank; the tube in my mouth feeds, hydrates, and oxygenates my blood and body. I know my eyes are open, but only because of the resistance that the gel puts on my eyelashes when I blink. Blinking five times in a row activates my heads-up display. The lasers inside each eyelid wink and draw a grid directly onto my retinas. Working my tongue around the tube, I reach the mouth-mouse. Each screen on the grid has the same message, "Your L.I.F.E. is temporarily suspended. Please standby." The date/time screen is even shut off. Midnight flashes in the upper-left corner, 1 JAN 2203 flashes in the upper right. It might be midnight, but it's certainly not New Year's Day of the year I was born.

Instrumental music starts playing in my head. Then, a woman's voice.

Please standby. All doctors are currently assisting other patients. A medical professional will be with you in the order you were revived. Your expected wait time is, the voice pauses, *less than two minutes. We appreciate your patience. Your business is very important to us. Please remain calm, and a doctor will be with you shortly.*

The music comes back. I can't remember why I am in a hospital or why the computer asked me the brain damage questions that everyone watches on television.

The woman's voice returns, the music plays softly in the background.

Did you know that since the inception of the Life-force Input and Feedback Equipment network, millions of lives have been saved? L.I.F.E. can alert paramedics in case of injury, heart attack, and stroke. L.I.F.E. can administer life-saving medication, while paramedics are in transit. And remember to visit the Gizmo store. Listen to your favorite radio stations, balance your checkbook, find show times, shop for groceries, or have a confidential chat with a personal counselor. The possibilities are endless. Ask your healthcare provider for authentic L.I.F.E. hardware and software. L.I.F.E., the one piece of equipment you cannot live without.

Every time I hear that commercial, I roll my eyes. When I had my annual service a few weeks ago, that commercial played continuously in the lobby's Muzak system. We all have it installed at birth, I wanted to shout. Immigrants must be retrofitted with a L.I.F.E. rig before they can receive citizenship. The government insists that everyone gets the required upgrades, and as our bodies change, the biometrics are resized for ease of use and comfort. I personally went through ten different mouth-mice before they found one that didn't leave a callus the size of a squash on my tongue.

They might as well urge me to drive a Vague Automobile or drink Ishmael's Coffee. We don't have a choice. There is no competition. Well, the big corporations, like Ishmael's and Vague, prop up shadow competitors, companies that distribute coffee and cars that both taste, and handle like, they were made of the same material, namely used toilet paper. But it's cheaper for them than a monopoly lawsuit.

The life of a competitor is an easy one. Never waiting on customers, never worrying about inventory, just sitting in your shop watching videos on BluTube and waiting for the monthly "profit" check to arrive from your "competitor." After retirement from the cubicle factory, when I've put in my forty years watching a machine install drawer hardware and am allowed to leave my X-class job, I intend to open a coffee shop, as a competitor to *Ishmael's*.

There's a vibration in the tank, as the music stops. A screen the size of my palm warms up several inches in front of my face, and a recorded female voice plays in my ear. *All interactions are recorded for quality assurance and use in our training.*

Then, a real male voice said, "Thank you for your patience, I'm Doctor D. Kiefer-G55. I'm going to turn the monitor on so you can see me. Give me a thumbs up for 'yes' and a thumbs down for 'no.'"

I put the thumb on my left hand up, and the doctor's mustached face appears. The screen is high-impact plastic, no thicker than my fingernail and floats freely in the gel.

"Try not to speak, or you may dislodge the tube and get a mouthful of gel. Just give me a thumbs up for good or thumbs down for bad. How are you feeling?"

Thumbs up.

"Good. I'm going to explain your injuries and do a few tests. If you do well, you'll be on your way home in no time. Okay?"

Thumbs up.

"Excellent. I'm going to override your L.I.F.E., so I can show you where you sustained injuries." The laser grid on my eyes shows a green outline of my body, parts flash red, as the doctor spoke. "You were dead for a few moments, as your skull was separated from your spine, eight of your vertebrae were crushed, likewise, your right arm and right leg were crushed entirely, your left shoulder was dislocated, your pelvis was fractured here, here, and here, and you had a pretty severe concussion. All that has been repaired, and we don't expect any complications. Okay?"

Thumbs up.

"Now, I'm going to test your reflexes. You may feel a slight prick, but just try to relax." An electrical impulse makes my right arm jerk, then my left, and then both legs. Likewise, each hand contracts, along with both feet, as the device, whatever it is, hovers through the tank. "Good. Reflexes are normal. I'm going to let some light into the tank now, so I can do a visual inspection. If you can't handle the light, just make a fist and I'll stop, okay?"

Thumbs up.

"Here we go."

Light slowly shines into the tank, and I can make out the room, full of similar tanks, some blackened, some empty. A few are transparent with doctors or nurses standing in front of them, holding clipboards, talking to floating patients contained therein. Dr. Kiefer-G55 is shorter than me, probably six foot, with dark hair parted over his right ear and a bushy mustache. He doesn't look up at me, just maneuvers the screen around the tank using the trackball on his clipboard. Apparently satisfied with what he viewed, the doctor brings the screen back in front of my face.

"Everything looks good. Do you have any questions?"

Thumbs up. The grid on my eye shows a list of questions, and I scroll down with my tongue to the first one that is relevant.

"An airborne container ship dropped a forty-ton Conex box on your conveyance," the doctor answered, after reading the question from his clipboard. "Fortunately, only one Conex box fell, and there was no one else on the road at the time."

I scroll to the next relevant question.

"You've been here for four days. We would have had you out in two days but reattaching your skull to your spine was a bit tricky, and we had to send for a specialist."

I absorb this information, then thought of one other question.

"Your attorney sued the company that owns the container ship. The negligent loadmaster was fired and faced civil and criminal charges. He was made to pay you thirty-million cred-its, a sum matched by the company, then the loadmaster was publicly executed two days ago. We hoped to have you at the execution for closure, but that was not possible. The execution is available to order on memory card in our gift shop, if you'd like a copy. It's also streaming on BluTube for the next 90 days, I believe. The container ship company, as a peace offering, also provided you with a new conveyance." The doctor scrolls down on his clipboard. "A brand new Vague," the face on the screen said with a wink. "A real beauty. Any other questions?"

Thumbs down.

"Okay, I'll get the nurse, and we'll get you discharged and on your way. Have a nice day." The screen didn't shut off when he called for the nurse. She was ten feet to the doctor's left, but he used the clipboard's vid-link to summon her. Another screen moves into position in front of my face, this one filled by the blonde nurse. "Nurse," the doctor said into his vid-link, "sedate this man, and start his discharge paperwork."

"Yes, doctor," the nurse said, as she walks up to take the doctor's place in front of my tank. The doctor's screen shuts off and retreats, as he walks to his next patient's tank. The nurse's screen centers itself in front of my face. "Good morning," she said, her smile taking up most of the screen. I give her a little wave. "I'm going to give you a sedative, so we can get you out of this tank. Your record indicates that you are not allergic to any medication. Is that true?"

Thumbs up.

"Okay, read through the warning that pops up, and I'll be back in a few minutes." The nurse looks familiar. She seems friendly, but her eyes dart back and forth as she spoke, reading from the script scrolling across her clipboard. When the nurse leaves, the grid displayed several hundred pages of warnings and disclaimers. I scroll to the bottom of the first page when I hear:

Doctor prescribed sedative, now dispensing.

My wrist vibrates as L.I.F.E. mixes different drugs into the sedative, then shoots the potent liquid into my artery. Just before consciousness leaves me, I realize that the nurse looks like my wife.

At Superior Patriotism, our specialty is making sure that you are driving the most patriotic car on the road. Custom bumper wraps and magnetic memorabilia to fit any vehicle and any budget. Ask about our subscription services. The look of your vehicle can be updated at your request or whenever new War on Terror commemorative designs become avail-

able. Remember, you aren't a Patriot until you visit Superior Patriotism.

G ravity and consciousness arrive at the same instant, and I jerk upright in the recovery room recliner. The grid appears in my vision.

Please standby while your L.I.F.E. initializes.

The status bar reaches one hundred percent, and I scroll through each screen to make sure I still have all my Gizmos installed. The date/time is correct, according to the clock on the wall. My planner is back online, as well as my email and phone. I had several messages, text and voice, from various relatives wishing me well. One message was from my boss. He told me to take a couple days off and come back when I was ready. My bank statement shows the deposit of the sixty million credits. The next item was the hospital's withdrawal of forty million credits for my stay, which put me at twenty million, and a Gizmo calculated that I could safely take three more days off from work before I got behind on my bills.

A button on my wrist deactivated the grid, and I began pulling my belongings from a box next to the chair. The hospital had cleaned my jumpsuit or replaced it. The nametape over the left breast pocket looked new, P. McGewan-X04 was stitched meticulously, along with my company's logo. The front of the jumpsuit closes automatically, once my feet and hands go through the appropriate openings. My boots conform to my feet, as I step into them. The only item remaining in the box is my universal identification card, which I place in my left breast pocket.

As I open the curtain to leave the recovery room, my wrist vibrates.

Please make your way to the Discharge desk located on this floor.

After several wrong turns, I activate the map Gizmo, and the grid points me in the right direction.

The woman sitting at the glass-encased Discharge desk doesn't look up. Her Terminal drops down from the ceiling on a retractable arm, causing a screeching sound in both of my ears.

"Name?" her image asks, as I take a step back.

"McGewan-X04." I expected some sort of reaction when I said 'X04.' A knowing smile to let me know that she had started out in a lowly X-class job and worked her way up to administrative specialist, the O-class. Alternatively, a grimace would let me know that the X-class was beneath her contempt. Instead, her face is blank. She probably discharges people from every class, every day and has no opinion one way, or the other.

A document appears on the side of her screen. "Read this, thumbprint where appropriate, sign at the bottom." I oblige her with four thumbprints on the margin and a scribbled signature with the stylus dangling from a string. "Your doctor has issued a prescription," she said, as her Terminal tries to get closer to me and make eye contact. The shrieking noise increases as the Terminal moves nearer, so I keep bobbing and ducking to keep clear of it. "The pharmacy is on the first floor. I'll send you a map. Have a nice day." She pivots away and takes aim at the man standing behind and to the right of me. "Name?"

Once I am away from the desk, the ringing or feedback or whatever it was stopped, but every doctor and nurse I pass in the hallway with a clipboard brings it back. My head begins to pound on the elevator ride to the lobby. Three doctors stood between me and the door to the first fifty floors, but I was alone for the rest of the trip.

There's a short line at the pharmacy. I zone out, trying to relax enough to stop my headache. The pharmacist's Terminal drops down from the ceiling, startling me visually and audibly, as a wave of static assaults me. I step around the screen and up to the counter.

"I have a prescription," I said directly to the man behind the counter. He looks down, sweat beading on his forehead, his hands shaking.

You are experiencing a panic attack. A mood stabilizer is being dispensed, and your personal counselor will be with you momentarily.

The med Gizmo on my wrist display shows that no medications are being administered.

The pharmacist's hands stop shaking after a moment, and he maneuvers his digital image in front of me again, the feedback screaming in my ears.

"The Sanitary Terminals are for everyone's protection, sir," said the face, as I stumble back. The man behind the counter mumbles to himself, while his recording deals with me. "What was your name, sir?"

"McGewan-Xo4," I said, keeping my distance from the Terminal.

"Please place your left wrist in the prescription tube," the man's head told me on the screen, as it led me to the appropriate tube. I place my left arm up to the elbow into the clear plastic. The tube seals above my elbow, and the pharmacist's Terminal moves on to help someone else.

Nothing happened. I watched as three people step up to other prescription tubes, got their prescriptions updated, upgraded, and integrated into their L.I.F.E., and then they left while I stood there.

I grew impatient, as nothing continued to happen at my particular tube. My headache intensified the longer I stood in the pharmacy. Wave upon wave of pain eroded the shores of my good humor. My ears and neck crisped with the anger that welled up inside me.

"Excuse me," I said, finally.

The Terminal turns to me from across the pharmacy. "Yes, sir?" asks the pharmacist's face.

"I know you're busy," I said, trying to keep the fury out of my voice, "but I have been standing here for almost twenty seconds, and nothing has happened."

"Oh, my word, sir," the pharmacist gushes on the screen, but far enough away that the screaming in my ears had stopped. The actual pharmacist quakes at the counter several paces away. The tremors seem to be shrinking him from the top down, until he became a haircut hovering at counter level. "I am so sorry, sir," said his disembodied face. "Let me see what's the matter."

Everything will be fine. Your superiors will most certainly take pity on you for a minor error.

"You think?" mumbles the actual pharmacist from approximately floor level.

Though, there is always a shortage of souls at the Molybdenum Mines, so try to be more diligent.

The actual pharmacist whimpers from under the counter.

"Well," said the confident face on the screen, "here's the problem. You're L.I.F.E. operating system is obsolete. No wonder nothing happened."

"Obsolete?" I ask. "I updated it five days ago."

"Five days? There's been two updates, four builds, and sixteen service packs in the last five days, sir. I couldn't possibly give you a prescription with such an antiquated operating system. You'll need to update or go without."

The prescription tube releases my arm to allow me to select the update on my wrist display. I scroll through the hundreds of pages of terms of service and end-user license agreements on my heads-up display, and at the bottom, agreed to the agreements by tonguing the 'Agree' button with my mouth-mouse. If I would have stood in the pharmacy for another full minute, I would have become most disagreeable.

"There," I said, as I jam my arm back into the prescription tube, until 'Download Complete' flashes on my heads-up display.

A mechanical arm releases my wrist display and I can see the mechanism imbedded in the working tissue of my arm. The delicate robot removes specific vials, adds different vials. In less than ten seconds, my prescription is filled. When the tube opens, the pharmacist's Terminal drops from the ceiling, right in front of me. "Would you like me to tell you the warnings for this prescription?"

"No," I said, as I attempt to leave the pharmacy. The noise in my ears continues, ebbing and surging, as I move away from the Terminal, while the pharmacist continues moving it toward me.

"Possible side effects?"

"No," I repeated.

"Drug interactions?"

"Just send it all to me. I have to go," I said, ducking under the Terminal.

Anti-depressant dispensing. As your personal counselor, I advise—but the voice trails off, as I run out onto the street.

The hospital's doors whisper closed behind me and I freeze in my tracks. Four days of sensory-deprivation, whether conscious or not, changes a person and I was unprepared for the noise and motion of the world. The buzzing in my head is still there, but the sea of voices drowns out most of it.

Standing motionless on the slab of concrete by the hospital's entrance, people sweep in and out of the hospital, keeping an arm's length from me. Everybody is in a hurry, heads down, concentrating on the five feet of slidewalk in front of them, shouting at their wrists. Dictating memos into their word processors. Negotiating business deals over the phone. Programming reminders into their organizers. Punching make-believe zombies on their heads-up display. Audio blogging about last night's reality show they watched. Shouting gibberish at themselves, the recipients of their tirades unseen.

The front of every building has a liquid billboard, giant television, or holographic image screaming advertisements down at the heedless masses. Ishmael's Coffee. The Flanery Defense. Vague Automotive.

My wrist buzzes after a few minutes, followed by the grid and a whisper in my head:

Your heart rate has increased, and your palms are perspiring. Would you care for a mood stabilizer?

I select, 'No,' with my tongue.

Perhaps a chat with your personal counselor?

'No,' again.

I step forward and wait for an opening on the slidewalk. It only takes a moment before I see a woman get off to my left, and then her vacated set of yellow footprints are under the soles of my boots, whisking me down the street.

Please standby, your consumer experience software is calibrating.

After a brief pause, the voice returns.

Based on recent activity, the following slidewalk ride is brought to you by the makers of prescription Chillaxafed.

A holo-cone shoots up around my feet, the world around me slightly opaque from the holographic images. Sweaty, shirtless men levering a railroad track into place, driving railway spikes into the ground in slow-mo.

War on Terror got you down?

The announcer's voice pipes directly into my head, but it screeches and hisses on my eardrums.

Constant fear of a fiery death wearing you out? Unable to focus at work because there might be a suicide bomb with your name on it? Ask your healthcare expert if prescription Chillaxafed is right for you. Physical alertness has never felt so mellow.

Calm.

Responsive.

Alert.

Productive.

Chillaxafed.

The Patriot's mood stabilizer.

Click 'Learn More' for more information.

Two buttons appear chest high in front of me. My fist strikes 'Dismiss' and the holo-cone to dissipate.

On my right, liquid billboards take up the first-floor windows of every building I pass. The looping video clips play, and every spokesperson's voice goes directly into my head, trying to get my attention. To my left, the slidewalk going the opposite direction whips shouting people past me. Beyond them, vehicles weave back and forth through the constant press of traffic.

Something's wrong, but over the buzz, billboards, traffic, and all those voices, I can't put my finger on it. I look up, the muscles in the back of my neck protesting, as I stare. The buildings seem to go on forever, bowing in toward one another across the street. A thin sliver of blue sky is barely visible, black dots—drones—circle in a constant holding pattern. One female voice makes its way to the front of my consciousness.

"You won't believe this. There's a guy just staring up at the sky."

What's he looking at? asks another woman.

"The sky, I guess."

Why?

"I don't know, but he isn't working or using a Gizmo. He's just riding the slidewalk in silence, staring at the sky. Like a psychopath."

That's creepy.

I look down, then to my left and right. Several other people on the slidewalk had looked up as well, trying to see what I was looking at. I turn to see the woman behind me.

"Oh, no, he's looking at me now."

Call the police, the voice tells her.

"Are you talking to a woman on the phone?" I ask.

"He's talking to me," the woman said, looking at my feet. "To me. Directly."

Hang up, and call the police, said the voice on the phone.

I stumble backwards, off the slidewalk, and into the first door that appears.

The recorded voice in my head thanks me for choosing Ishmael's, but the buzz distorts the name, the 's' at the end continues for several seconds.

A Terminal runs across its tracks to meet me at the door. "Welcome to Ishmael's," said the perky, young woman with a flourish of what I could see of her hair. "Would you care to try our new Mocha Monkey in a commemorative mug? All proceeds from the sale of the mugs go to the survivors and victims' families of the tragedy." A picture of the drink appears next to her face. The picture is small, but the mug seems to depict giant blocks crushing cars with the legend, "Forever Remembered."

"What tragedy?" I ask, gritting my teeth as the feedback buffets my eardrums.

She blinks several times, jerks her head side-to-side, moving the camera to stay centered on her face. "What tragedy? Where have you been? Terrorists hijacked a container ship last week and dropped dozens of forty-ton boxes onto people on the freeway. It's only been all over the news for the last four days."

"I've been in the hospital for the last...four..." I said, only to stop, as the wheels in my head spin. The headline scrolling across the nearest newspaper states something about a sole survivor being released from the hospital that morning. When I look up, I stare at the back of the Terminal. The woman turns to look at the newspaper, as well. She pivots the screen, until I can see her face again.

"You're him, aren't you?" she asks, her eyes wide. "You're the sole survivor!"

People turn their wrist cameras toward me, relaying an image to their eye, no doubt recording it for later.

"No, no," I said, "I'm the sole victim of an entirely different circumstance. Just came in for a coffee."

"No, you're him. I saw your picture on the one-hour special."

Without warning, two voices come into my head, one male, one female, but both say the same thing in un-synched stereo.

Talking to, looking at, or following someone, especially a person of celebrated status, is stalking and not allowed by law.

I glance around at all the wrists pointed at me and wonder who had thought about stalking me, and more importantly, why I could hear their personal counselors. Then, the perky coffee employee's words sink in, so I turn my attention back to her.

"One-hour special? About what?"

"About your struggle to survive the vicious terrorist attack, your will to live in spite of insurmountable odds, your..."

"Wait," I said, waving my hands in front of her face, "my whole life wouldn't fill up an hour of television, let alone the minor car accident I got in to. I'm sorry, but you've got the wrong guy."

"I know it's you," she said, her eyes red, tears dropping onto each cheek. "I know it's you. Excuse me." Her face shoots into the ceiling and vanishes. At the back of the room, I see a lone figure run through a door marked, *Employees Only*. I slowly turn and stare down each camera pointed at me, until everybody goes back to their USA Tomorrows and Grande Mocha Monkeys in the Forever Remembered commemorative mugs. I stand there for a while, thinking, wondering if terrorists had, in fact, dropped the container onto my car.

A tone starts in my ears, as televisions drop from the ceiling. Each customer snaps their head up to stare at the flatscreens.

The voice in my head, distorted by feedback, said, *The following Presidential Address is brought to you by Ishmael's. The Patriot's coffee. Now, an important message from the President of the United States, Matthias Jackson.* The Ishmael's logo fades out, and the Presidential Seal appears on the screen, then fades out as well, to show the President sitting behind his desk in the Oval Office.

"My fellow Americans..."

I double over in agony at the sound of President Jackson's voice saying, "...eight minutes ago, Eastern Standard Time, excuse me..."

President Jackson clears his throat and takes a sip of water, his lips touching the water sounds like a tidal wave crashing into my skull. "Eight minutes ago, at 8:05 a.m., Eastern Standard Time, the Hermod shoe factory outside Knoxville, Tennessee, was bombed by terrorists."

Plugging my ears only makes the buzzing worse as President Jackson continues to speak.

"No survivors have been found at this time, but a terrorist organization in Madagascar has taken responsibility for this heinous attack against America. We cannot allow such attacks on American soil to go unpunished."

I try to induce hyperventilation, remembering a news blurb about terrorists surviving torture through this practice.

"As we speak, a bill is on the Congressional floor, which will allow us to implement measures to defend this great country of ours. These measures will prevent such assaults against Americans from happening in the future. As good American citizens, we all must unite in this cause."

Practice is what I need, as the faux hyperventilation has no effect on the treble staff grinding through my eardrums.

"Every American, regardless of race, religion, or creed, must stand together, as Christian Americans. I know that I speak for all Americans when I say to the survivors and families of the victims of this attack, America will never forget the price you paid today. Thank you, and may the Lord be with you." President Jackson's face is replaced by the Presidential Seal. After a moment, the seal fades into another room.

"No, thank *you*," I mumble, as the screaming pain recedes, and I can take a normal breath.

The President's press secretary stands behind a podium, an American flag to either side of him. "I will now answer questions regarding President Jackson's address."

I shake my head, hold my breath, and flex every muscle in my body, as my ears take another beating. The camera pulls back to show the press secretary standing in front of a six-foot square screen. The outlines of hundreds of small boxes fill the screen, tiny faces visible in each through my half-open, tense eyelids. "Yes," said the press secretary, randomly touching one of the boxes to enlarge it and take up most of the screen space. A reporter's face is identifiable, though transparent for a moment. People in the control booth switch perspective to the reporter sitting behind a desk, taking up the entire television screen.

"T. DeVore-Y16, *New York Times*. Exactly what are these defensive measures President Jackson spoke of?"

The cameras cut back to the press secretary. "As Americans, we are protected by the Lord Jesus Christ..."

"Amen." Everyone in the coffee shop mumbles aloud.

"...and two hundred thousand modified B-1200 Stealth Velociraptor Unmanned Drone Bombers. These drones are equipped with scanners that detect any explosive materials throughout the country. If explosives are detected, the drones will engage and vaporize the terrorists with pinpoint accuracy, along with anyone within a half-mile radius of said terrorists. This is a temporary measure, under the Articles of War on

Terror, until the law passes unanimously through both houses of Congress, making it a full-time defensive provision. Next question. Yes?"

The reporter's cube shrinks and is quickly replaced by another, a woman this time.

"J. Callen-Y25, *San Francisco Chronicle*. Isn't having B-1200 Stealth Velociraptor Unmanned Drone Bombers flying over our homes, twenty-four hours a day an invasion of privacy?"

The press secretary rolls his eyes and said, "Americans will understand that having modified, and I must stress this, *modified* B-1200 Stealth Velociraptor Unmanned Drone Bombers flying over our cities, is a necessary precaution to protect their lives and the lives of their loved ones. Yes?"

Suddenly, a different woman's face takes up the screen. "D. Noffsinger-Y37, *Miami Herald*. Are there plans for an invasion of Madagascar?"

"There are no plans, at this time, to physically invade Madagascar. An investigation is under way, and I am certain there will be reprisals for this attack on many levels. That is all. The Lord be with you." The screen went black and retracts into the ceiling.

I relax and take a deep breath, the blood returning to my head. A babble of voices, male and female personal counselors, invade my thoughts before the television screens are out of sight.

Are you having a panic attack?

There is no reason to be frightened.

Would a mood stabilizer help lower your heart rate?

Mood stabilizer now being dispensed.

Your personal advisor will be with you momentarily, please remain calm.

You have exceeded your maximum daily allowance of mood

stabilizers. Paramedics have been notified, and a sedative is being dispensed.

A ripple effect ensues. Shoulders slump in a wave, past me, and continue across the room. One man went beyond slumped shoulders, banging his head on a table as he lost consciousness. His commemorative mug barely beats him to the floor. No one seems to notice, other than me.

My wrist glows green. Heart rate, blood pressure, breathing, sweating, muscle tension, all normal with no medication dispensed. I feel a wave of pride by dealing with the latest tragedy so well.

If I could just get a cup of coffee and find my car, I could go home, I thought. It dawned on me that I had probably scared off the only employee.

I decide to walk up to the counter. Ten seconds pass with my palms flat on the counter, glancing around for an *Ishmael's* barista. My eyes scan the toll-free "How are we doing?" sign. Last week, I would have dialed the number after five seconds and had the entire staff fired before I finished my cup of coffee, but today, I am full of forgiveness. I am about to clear my throat and ask for help when a Terminal drops from the ceiling, hitting me squarely between the eyes. Eventually, I wake up, on my back, with a screen wavering in and out of focus above me.

"Are you okay, sir?" said the boy's face.

I work my jaw side to side, wiggle a finger in each ear, and take a deep breath. The buzzing is gone. "I think that did the trick."

"I'm glad I could be of assistance," said the boy, unfazed by my non sequitur. "Can I assist you further?"

"Just a Mocha Monkey in the commemorative mug, and I'll be good to go," I said, still lying on the floor.

"I'm sorry, sir. The Mocha Monkey is not currently available in a commemorative mug. Would you like a Mocha

Monkey in a regular cup, or would you prefer a Jumpin' Java Jive in the Never Forgotten commemorative mug?" A drink appears next to the boy's face, spinning slowly to show the Hermod Winged Spear, an illustration of an explosion, and, if my geography is correct, the outline of Tennessee.

"How long was I unconscious?" I ask, standing up.

"Only a few seconds, sir," he replies, as the Terminal moves out of my way.

"I'd really like one of the Forever Remembered mugs. I may have been involved in that incident, and..." I stop brushing the legs of my jumpsuit and try to give him a look, using whatever alleged celebrity status I had left.

"Which mug, sir?"

"You know, the one with blocks crushing cars on it."

"I'm sorry, sir?" he said, shrugging. The face on the screen is clean-shaven and devoid of adornments, but the actual person behind the counter is covered in facial tattoos and has a two-foot neon pink goatee.

"The Mocha Monkey was just in it when I came in."

"Oh, that mug. I'm sorry, sir. The old mugs were destroyed and recycled immediately to make way for the new mugs, you understand." I didn't, but I nodded anyway. "So, would you prefer the Mocha Monkey or Triple J in the commemorative mug, sir?"

"I don't know. Which one's better?"

He gives me a blank stare.

"Which do you prefer?" I ask him.

Silence.

"Which one has darker coffee in it?"

He hesitates, but then said, "The Mocha Monkey has Freedom Roasted Coffee in it."

"Fine. Grande Mocha Monkey."

"Are you sure, sir? I'm not allowed to put that in a

commemorative mug."

"You know what? You're right, make it an Enormetron Mocha Monkey. It's a long drive home."

"Anything else, sir?" asks the boy, smiling at me.

"That's it. No, wait," I said, "lots of sprinkles and that should be it."

The boy's face falls. He gave me a moment to reconsider, then his eyes glazed as his heads-up display pops up. His jaw moves side to side, as he works his mouth-mouse to activate the machine in front of him. The automated espresso machine whirs to life, steams, and *praps*, as I authorize the charge with my thumbprint on the Terminal.

A plain, white cup appears in front of me a moment later. "Thanks," I said to the boy. As I turn to leave, every customer has their wrist aimed at me, again, as I take the first sip of my drink. I slowly walk out of the coffee shop, trying to watch everyone in my periphery, their wrists tracking my progress.

Terrorist Tip Line, how can I help you help all of us?
Terrorist Tip Line, how can I help you help all of us?
Terrorist Tip Line, how can I help you help all of us?
Terrorist Tip Line, how can I help you help all of us?

The coffee cup is still to my lips, when the doors part and let me onto the street.

At Ishmael's, we know you're busy. We know the need for an Ishmael's can strike at any moment. We know you. With more than forty-eight thousand locations in the greater metropolitan area, Ishmael's is always right around the corner.

Which corner?

Every corner.

Ishmael's.

The Patriot's Coffee Shop.

ABOUT THE AUTHOR_

Jason R. Richter is a perennial runner-up in Jason R. Richter look-alike contests. The orphaned love child of Kilgore Trout and Margaret Dumont, he was raised by marauding gypsy accountants. When the bottom fell out of the interplanetary death ray market at the dawn of the new millennium, he turned his hobby (a game he calls "Lies to Strangers") into a career. He currently lives.

To stay up to date with whatever nonsense Jason is up to, visit DiskordianPress.com/Newsletter

If you find typos or errors of any sort, please email us at:
  Trouble@DiskordianPress.com

Otherwise, thanks for reading. A review on Goodreads, Amazon, or wherever you read book reviews goes a long way to support independent authors. Cheers!